STRANGEWAYS TO OLDHAM
(The Most Efficient Route to Eternity)

The Belchester Chronicles: 1

A Lady Amanda Golightly Murder Mystery

ANDREA FRAZER

Strangeways to Oldham

ISBN 9781783756469

Copyright © 2012 by Andrea Frazer

This edition published by Accent Press 2014

The right of Andrea Frazer to be identified as the Author of the Work has been asserted by her in accordance with the Copyright, Designs and Patents Act, 1988

For the Campbell family in New Zealand.
They know why!

Other books by Andrea Frazer

<u>Falconer Files</u>

Death of an Old Git
Choked Off
Inkier than the Sword
Pascal Passion
Murder at the Manse
Music to Die For
Strict and Peculiar
Christmas Mourning
Grave Stones
Death in High Circles
Glass House

<u>Others</u>

Choral Mayhem

DRAMATIS PERSONAE

Anstruther, Dr – elderly GP

Beauchamp – butler and general factotum at Belchester Towers

Campbell, Dr Andrew – new, young GP

Cholmondley-Crichton-Crump, Hugo – a permanent house guest at Belchester Towers

Edwards, Malcolm – head of a private nursing service

Foster, Derek – a care worker

Golightly, Lady Amanda – owner of Belchester Towers

Matron – head of the Birdlings Serenade Nursing Home, whose name is known to no one

Myers, Richard – an elderly local resident

Pagnell, Reginald – a resident of the Birdlings Serenade Nursing Home

Plunkett, Nurse Sarah – an employee at the Birdlings Serenade Nursing Home

Tweedie, Enid – cleaner, friend, and co-conspirator of Lady Amanda

Updyke, Dr Cedric – an orthopaedic consultant at Belchester City Hospital

Williams, Young Mr – an elderly partner of Freeman Hardy, Williams and Williams

Police Personnel

Inspector Moody

PC Adrian Glenister

A NOTE ON PRONUNCIATION

Beauchamp's name is usually pronounced Beecham in England, but Lady Amanda insists on the French pronunciation, Bo-sham.

Hugo's surnames are pronounced Chumley-Cryten-Crump.

PROLOGUE

Belchester was a small cathedral city, about fifteen miles from the south coast; the largest dwelling in its environs Belchester Towers. Belchester Towers had been built in the early nineteenth century by one Godfrey Golightly, nouveau riche, and out to display his newly found wealth.

That the man had no taste or breeding mattered not a jot to him, and he celebrated his recently acquired title with a heap of a red-brick building, ugly, four-square, with a huge crenellated tower at each corner and a faux moat surrounding the whole – a raspberry to all the other fine houses that had a wealth of history behind them.

Godfrey Golightly would build his own dynasty, and his house would mature into its surroundings over time, of this he had had no doubt.

In the last almost two hundred years, the fortunes of the Golightly family had fluctuated, down to the present day, and last member of the direct line of descent, Lady Amanda, who was now of a certain age – i.e. wouldn't tell anyone that she had recently become the recipient of a state pension. She lived there with only the company of a general factotum called Beauchamp, and an army of casual cleaners and gardeners, whom the aforementioned Beauchamp summoned at intervals, as and when they were needed, to turn the dwelling back into a decent place in which to live.

Lady Amanda's parents had been killed in an accident on the London to Brighton Rally some years before, after driving straight into a tree. They had been drunk to the wide due to frequent nips from their hip-flasks of cocktails, and Lady Amanda considered that there could not have been a better way for them to go.

The car behind had said they were laughing their heads off at the time of the accident, after 'Daddy', as she always thought of her father, had lost control of the steering. It was considered not to be speed that had been the main cause of their death, because the old car didn't have it in her to go very fast, more the sheer bad luck that they had both broken their necks and fractured their skulls when they had been thrown from the body of the vehicle, face first, into said venerable and unmovable tree.

Lady Amanda was an aficionado of cocktails; in fact, she had been since she was a teenager, having been brought up with them, one could say, and she hoped that she had a suitably bizarre and fun ending – if death can ever be fun! – to her own life, when the time eventually arrived.

A formidable character, she conducted her life openly and honestly, and would have no truck with slyness, prevarication, untruths, or any hole-in-the-corner, or cloak-and-dagger behaviour. She was hardest of all on bad manners, and would not tolerate them from anyone, no matter what their station in life. Being a blunt woman, however, Lady Amanda called a spade 'a bloody shovel' if she didn't call it 'trumps', although she very rarely used coarse language and frowned upon it in others.

Physically, she bore no relationship to the figure that most imagined, having only heard her name. She was not tall and willowy, a waif – a go-lightly, in fact, whom a gust of wind would bowl over. Instead, she was short and squat – what she liked to refer to as portly, where others said she was just fat – with piercing green eyes, and blond curls.

Her hair was her only vanity, but more of that later …

Chapter One

'Beauchamp!'

The name was shouted in a glass-shattering screech, which echoed round the vast entrance hall of Belchester Towers. 'Beauchamp! Where the dickens are you! Come here, at once! Beauchamp!'

Thus, she summoned the one and only other occupier of her vast house. She was standing now, in the entrance hall, holding a piece of paper in her hands; holding it at arm's length and squinting furiously at it.

'How may I be of assistance, my lady?' Beauchamp had appeared at her side as if by magic, his footsteps silent as always on the stone-flagged floor. Lady Amanda didn't know how he did it, but he had often caused her to jump nearly out of her skin, with this inexplicable trick of his, to move around like a shade, with no intimation at all that he was near her. He was just, suddenly, there.

'What, in heaven's name, is this?' she demanded, thrusting the piece of paper in his face, without preamble.

Beauchamp took the proffered document, and scrutinised it in detail. 'It would appear to be a fine for speeding, my lady,' he informed his enraged mistress.

'Just what I thought, but how the devil can it be? I haven't had the Rolls out for ages. The thing's covered in dust and cobwebs, out there in the stables.' She followed this with a noise that it is only possible to write thus: 'Hrmph!'

'It does not concern the Rolls, my lady – it is, in fact, a notice for speeding on your tricycle.'

'My tricycle? Absolute rot! How could I possibly have

been speeding on my trike? Don't know what the world's coming to, when a respectable woman can't even ride her own trike without breaking the law. It's a load of absolute rot, Beauchamp, and I shall phone the Chief Constable about it. His father used to be a good friend of Daddy's, you know.'

'I fear that would do little good, my lady. It states here that you were travelling along the entrance road to the hospital, where the speed limit is only five miles an hour, and you nearly 'had' the senior orthopaedic consultant with your conveyance.'

Ignoring him completely, she continued, 'I mean, what sort of damage can one do, with a tricycle?'

Beauchamp eyed Lady Amanda's generous figure up and down, considered the weight of the ancient machine she had been propelling, and decided not to voice his conclusion, which was 'a considerable amount'. 'And the gentleman mentioned, my lady?' he prompted her to further explanation.

'He got out of the way in time, didn't he? I didn't exactly hit him!'

'No, but he only escaped being hit by your trike, by jumping off the entrance way into a rose bush, thus sustaining considerable damage to the material of his shirt and trousers, and a number of small scratches and abrasions.'

'Piffle!' retorted Lady Amanda, her face bearing a mutinous expression with which Beauchamp was only too familiar.

'The accompanying letter says that you didn't even stop to see how the poor man was.'

'I was late for visiting. Old Enid Tweedie, you know. How ridiculous, having to have her tonsils out at her age. Absolutely shaming, if you ask me. It's the sort of thing that children have done, then get a week of ice-cream and jelly until the pain goes away. Had it done myself, as a

4

matter of fact, when I was about seven. And then, a couple of weeks later, she had to go back in to have her gall bladder removed. There'll be nothing left of her, if she keeps having bits taken out at this rate.'

'It also says here, that you are lucky not to be charged with what is referred to in common parlance as "hit-and-run".'

'With a tricycle?' she shrilled, her voice rising with indignation. 'I shall dispute it, of course!'

'There were witnesses, my lady. I think they've got you by the proverbial "short and curlies",', Beauchamp informed her calmly. He was used to her moods by now, and didn't let it disturb him, even when she threw a first-class tantrum.

'Don't be coarse, Beauchamp!'

'Sorry, my lady.'

'So, what do I have to do now?' she asked him, her colour subsiding a little, as she realised she could probably leave this to Beauchamp to deal with, as he did with most things that arose in the household which required thought.

'I suggest that you just pay your fine like a model citizen, my lady, and bear in mind the speed limit in future. Mrs Tweedie wouldn't have been the worse for you arriving just a minute or two later, and you wouldn't have found yourself in this situation if you had observed the roadside speed limit signs.'

'Very well, Beauchamp. Get on with it.'

'There's just one more thing, my lady,' he asked.

'And what's that?'

'My name is pronounced Beecham, not that French variation you have used for some years now.'

'I'm sorry, Beauchamp, but your name is an ancient one that came over with the Conquest, and I cannot find it in myself to use its Anglicisation. Take it or leave it! You should be proud to bear such an ancient name!'

It was a long-running battle between them, and

Beauchamp gave in with a good grace, the way he always did, but one day – one day, he might just persuade her. And pigs would fly across a blue moon, when that happened, was his last thought on the matter.

'I'm going out this afternoon, on the trike, but I shall take what you've said into consideration. Enid Tweedie informed me, as best as she could, of course, with her throat being so sore, that old Reggie Pagnell has gone into a nursing home.

'Poor old thing! I haven't seen him in absolutely yonks! I expect he was before your time, but he and Daddy used to be business partners when I was a wee one.'

The thought of Lady Amanda ever being a 'wee one' made Beauchamp wince, but he managed to make it a mental wince that didn't appear on his features, lest his employer decided to take offence.

'Anyway, I thought I'd tricycle over there this afternoon, and see how he is; cheer him up; you know, that sort of thing?'

Beauchamp knew that some people were only too delighted to have the pleasure of Lady Amanda's company, and would gladly have run up a flag if they knew she were coming to visit. Others were not quite so fond of her, and were more likely to run up a side street at the rumour of a visit from her, but he maintained a respectful silence, knowing which side his bank account was buttered.

'Perhaps you would be good enough to get the old steed out for me, Beauchamp. Just leave it round the front, as usual, and check the horn, to make sure its bulb hasn't dozed.' Attached to the handlebars of the tricycle that used to be her mother's was a small version of an old-fashioned car horn, brass with a rubber bulb, and she was always worried that the rubber might have deteriorated to the point where she couldn't use it any more.

In fact, she had used it, she remembered, when that

chappie at the hospital had got in her way, and it had been in fine fettle then. Remembering this, she went to prepare for her visit with a smile on her face, hoping it would be a long time yet before she had to resort to one of those horrible little bell thingummyjigs.

Belchester was less than a mile away, now, as the little city's suburbs crept ever-increasingly outwards, towards Belchester Towers, and it was a relatively short ride for Lady Amanda to the Birdlings Serenade Nursing Home, (Nursing & Convalescence Our Speciality. Enquire about respite care), next to St Anselm's Church, and on the city's old northern border, just south of the cathedral.

She had never visited the place before, but surveyed in dismay its surroundings. To the west of the nursing home lay St Anselm's, and its beckoning graveyard. To its north was the city hospital, and, to the east, a doctor's and a dentist's surgery. The poor residents were surrounded on all sides by decay, illness and death, and it must be very depressing for them, she thought, as she propelled her tricycle, at a snail's pace, given what had occurred previously, up its drive to the main entrance.

The reception area that greeted her reminded her of how lucky she was not to be reduced by health and finances to live in a place like this. Despite the scents of polish and disinfectant, there lingered the odour of boiling greens and, underneath everything, a decided tang of urine, which made her wrinkle her nose in distaste. To think of poor Reggie Pagnell, ending up here.

At the desk, she announced in a booming voice that she had come to visit an old family friend, but when she announced that friend's name, the receptionist turned a little pale, and asked her if she'd wait, so that she could check with Matron, whether that would be all right or not.

'Stuff and nonsense!' declared Lady Amanda, watching the woman walk off down a corridor to her right, and then, consulting a handy list of residents, which had been pinned to the wall to the side of the desk, she spotted her target's room number, and toddled off down the left-hand corridor, in search of her father's old partner. Her eyesight was still good enough to read things at a distance, and she had learned all she needed to know. What did the woman want to involve Matron for?

Room number five was only a few steps away, and she gave a brisk knock on the door, and entered it hurriedly before that interfering receptionist woman came back with some excuse or other about why she couldn't pop in on poor old Reggie. Closing the door carefully behind her, she turned, ready to greet a familiar face, and was staggered to note that he wasn't tucked up in bed, as she had expected, but rather was laid out; the whole length of him, including his face, covered with a white sheet.

Startled into silence, she approached the shrouded figure almost on tiptoes, noticing as she did so that his bedside table bore two cocktail glasses, both of them empty. That was odd! She wouldn't have expected cocktails to have been served in a place like this. Almost instinctively, she bent her nose to the nearest glass, and gave a very unladylike sniff, then moved on to the other glass.

The first had smelled the same as the second, and she knew she recognised it, but could not put a name to it, off the top of her head. Her long experience of imbibing cocktails meant that she had an encyclopaedic knowledge of just about every cocktail that existed, and she knew she had come across this one before. Without even thinking about it, she placed one of the glasses in her capacious handbag, noticing, at the same time, that some liquid had recently been spilt on the carpet, in front of the cabinet.

Without a trace of embarrassment, she got down on all fours, and leant her nose towards the still-damp stain. Another gargantuan sniff confirmed what she had suspected she would find. This, too, was a recognisable cocktail, but there was something else there in the background, which she had detected in the glasses too.

Her thought were interrupted, however, as, at that moment, the door sprang open, and a whippet of a woman with an angry face confronted her. 'Who are you? And what the devil are you doing in here?' she barked, furiously.

Still on all fours, her forearms flattened before her as she bent forward, her nose almost touching the carpet, she thought furiously. 'I'm praying to Mecca, for the soul of the departed,' Lady Amanda improvised, in double-quick time. 'And, if it comes to that, who the devil are you?'

'I think you'll find that east is in the opposite direction, madam. I am Matron of this home, and you had no right to enter this room. The patients' privacy is secondary only to their welfare,' Matron yapped, looking at Mr Pagnell's strange visitor.

'In that case, why is poor old Reggie dead?' she asked, piercing the woman with a gimlet eye.

'He passed away not half an hour ago, and the doctor hasn't arrived yet to issue the certificate, although what business it is of yours, I haven't a clue. Who the devil are you, madam?'

'I,' began Lady Amanda, rising ponderously from the floor, and pulling herself up to her full height of five feet four, with the aid of the bed frame, 'am Lady Amanda Golightly of Golightly Towers.' That usually did it. The woman would be quelled now.

But she wasn't. 'I don't care if you're the Duchess of Cornwall. You can't just come waltzing into the private room of one of my residents without a by-your-leave. Now, I insist that you vacate this room this instant. You had no right to be here in the first place.'

'I didn't realise this was a prison,' Lady Amanda threw back at her. 'I thought this was a home, and one can have visitors at one's home, can't one?'

'Not without my say so,' spat Matron, sure that she had made her point this time.

As if to indicate the end of round one, a male voice called plaintively from a few doors down the corridor, 'Nurse! Nurse! I haven't had my tablets yet!'

The timbre of the voice registered in Lady Amanda's subconscious first, speeding through the twists and turns of Memory Lane at the speed of light, back on down it to her youth, and before she even realised what had just transferred itself to her conscious mind, yelled, 'Chummy!' and did an abrupt about-turn, to leave the room, and march purposefully towards the place whence the voice had sounded.

Through the doorway of a room on the other side of the corridor, the owner of the voice looked her up and down, and enquired, 'Manda?' unbelievingly.

'Chummy!' she hooted again, approaching the figure in a wing chair beside the window. 'Well, bless my soul, if it isn't old triple-barrelled Hugo! What the blue blazes are you doing in a place like this?'

'So it is you after all! I heard you bellowing at that old witch of a matron, and I thought, "good for you". It certainly sounded like you, but I couldn't believe it could possibly *be* you, not after all this time.'

'But what are you doing here?' asked Lady Amanda, hardly able to believe her eyes, that the elderly man she was looking at was the friend she hadn't seen for decades.

'It's the arthritis that got me, Manda. I had to have someone in to look after me a few times a week, and then it got even worse, until I just couldn't cope on my own any more, so I put myself in here. God's waiting room, we all call it. And that matron! What a gorgon! The old besom calls me Mr Cholmondley-Crichton-Crump! I've tried explaining to her that it's pronounced Chummley-Crighton, but she won't listen to me – thinks I'm in my dotage, just because I have difficulty in moving around.'

'Oh, how ghastly for you, you poor old thing! What an ignorant woman, and such bad manners to keep on doing it, after she's been corrected. I have the same trouble with my Beauchamp – you must remember him from the old days. He insists that his name is Beecham, and won't listen to a word I say on the subject. Well, I'm not standing for you being subject to that sort of thing! I'm getting you out of here. You simply can't stay. And whatever's happened to the house? Lovely old place!'

'I've got it on the market. Can't afford to stay here for long, at the prices they charge. I'm not made of savings, you know.'

'Just precisely what is the fee, per month, Hugo?' asked his visitor, with genuine interest.

At this question, he gestured her towards him, so that he could whisper in her ear.

'*Combien*, Hugo? How much?' she shouted, scandalised at the figure he had named. 'That does it, Chummy! You're moving into The Towers today. I can't think of you incarcerated in here for another day.'

'But how are you going to get me out,' asked Hugo, rather pathetically.

'I'm going to see that dried-up old hag, and get her to prepare your paperwork for you to leave, then I'm going back to The Towers to fetch the Rolls, before driving back here and moving you out, bag and baggage.'

'But how am I going to manage?' queried Hugo. 'You know, the nursing and helping side of it?'

'You'll have me and you'll have Beauchamp. If you're not paying out a fortune every month to stay in this urine-drenched prison, you can afford to have someone in, like you used to, for whenever it's necessary. I know The Towers isn't the most luxurious of homes, but it's got to be better than this.'

'A bed of nails in a pig sty would be better than this,

Manda. Do you really think you could swing it with old Mato?'

'Course I can. I'm still the gal I used to be, and I was a match for anyone in my youth.'

Lady Amanda Golightly treated everyone in life equally, no matter what their station, and had not yet met her Waterloo. That woman – that Matron person – had three strikes, then she was out. Those were the rules. She had had her first one, when she had been so rude to Lady Amanda, on finding her in Reggie Pagnell's room. Strike one! She had, even after repeated requests, refused to acknowledge the proper pronunciation of Hugo's rather protracted surname. Strike two! This would be her last chance.

With the light of battle in her eyes, that Hugo remembered of old, she marched out of his room, calling, 'Matron! Matron! I need to speak to you. *Now*, you wretched woman!'

For the next ten minutes, Hugo Cholmondley-Crichton-Crump was aware of raised voices, coming down the corridor to his room from the reception desk, and sat, quivering, wondering what was going on; what was being said about him, and where he'd be sleeping tonight. If it was to be here again, he knew he was probably in for a very rough time. Matron didn't like her word being questioned, let alone completely trampled over, and he knew his Manda of old.

When the disagreement, argument, fight – whatever it had been – had ended, Hugo heard brisk footsteps approaching his door from the corridor, and cowered down in his chair. Ooh-er, he was probably for it, now!

Lady Amanda erupted into his room, her appearance as sudden as that of a pantomime demon that had just shot up through a trapdoor in the floor. 'Did you know Reggie Pagnell was in here?' she asked, quite inconsequentially in Hugo's opinion, and when he answered in the affirmative, she nodded her head in approval, then told him, 'Right, that's all settled then.'

'What's all settled, Manda? I can't keep up with you.'

'You never could, Chummy, and I'm afraid you never will. That's it! I've sprung you! You're free to go! I've phoned Beauchamp on my mobile, and he says he'll fix the old trailer on to the Rolls, and come down to fetch us. You're coming to live with me, in Belchester Towers, and I won't hear a word to the contrary. Now, let's get your stuff packed.'

'Thank God!' said Hugo, on a loud sighing exhalation of breath.

'Thank *me*, if you please,' replied Lady Amanda, already pulling a suitcase from the top of the wardrobe. 'I shall also be telephoning round the local estate agents with reference to your house. I don't see why you should have to sell it, when it can bring you a perfectly good income. We'll get them to assess it for rent, and you can let it out – let it work for you, with a little something to make you more comfortable. Of course, if, when the property market rises again, you want to go for the lump sum, that's completely your affair. But nobody but a fool sells at the moment, Hugo, dear. Prices are so low. And now you won't have to line the pockets of the shysters who run this place any more.'

'I simply don't know how you do it. You're like a whirlwind, still. I would've considered that, after all these years, you might have slowed down a bit, but you've still got all the get up and go you had when you were a gal.'

'I have Hugo; it just takes me longer to recover from one of my tornados, now.'

Chapter Two

After settling Hugo into a suitable room on the ground floor, Lady Amanda and he took afternoon tea in the drawing room, as she explained Beauchamp's current job description to him.

'Bertie Wooster had Jeeves, Lord Peter Wimsey had Bunter; I have Beauchamp, who does his level best to live up to the impeccable record of his fictional counterparts. He's a sort of old family retainer-of-all-work. He seems to be good at absolutely everything, except the appreciation and pronunciation of his own name. I believe you met him first when he was Daddy's butler?'

At that moment, Beauchamp appeared in the doorway, silently as usual, to enquire about supper. 'What have you planned for us this evening? I know it's short notice, to feed another mouth, but we'll have to manage,' she enquired. 'You remember old Hugo, don't you?'

'Of course, my lady. Good evening, Mr Hugo. Nice to see you at Belchester Towers again, after all these years.' He turned to Lady Amanda. 'I had planned Dover sole, new potatoes, and a green salad,' Beauchamp intoned. He did a lot of intoning, when they had guests, she'd noticed.

'Stuff and nonsense!' she replied. 'Deal with the fish the best you can to feed three. Chuck it in some batter, chip the potatoes, and we can have it all fried, with some baked beans. My secret supply is in the camphor-wood coffer in my bedroom, Beauchamp.'

'I know, my lady. Thank you, my lady. Will there be anything else with that?'

'Yes. A pot of really strong Assam, a plate of white

sliced bread, suitably buttered, and lashings of tomato ketchup, thank you, Beauchamp. And we'll have a nice kipper for breakfast. Fried, mind – none of that grilled nonsense! You may go.'

'Thank you, my lady.' Beauchamp melted back through the doorway, and it closed without a sound.

'He's a bit unnerving, isn't he, Manda?' commented Hugo, having noticed the noiseless arrival and departure. 'I'd forgotten all about that trick of his, moving around without a sound.'

'Oh, Beauchamp's all right. Started here as a boot boy, donkey's years ago, and worked his way up, until he was the only one left. Serves him right! Haha! Good old stick, though, Beauchamp. Would trust him with my life,' she finished, full of the man's praises, even though the two of them often fell out.

'Loyalty! That's what it all comes down to in the end: loyalty, Hugo. And talking of loyalty, tell me about Reggie Pagnell. Did you see much of him in Stalag Birdlings – the place even has a sickening name!'

'Not really, Manda. He was in quite a bad way. Marbles gone, you know. I tried popping into his room, when I realised he was in there too, but he didn't have a clue who I was, so I stopped going. Too depressing, making me think that I was headed there too.'

'Tommyrot, Chummy! You'll still be compos mentis when we're all gaga! Now, back to Reggie – did he have any visitors?'

'Only the one, that I'm aware of. Came once a month, for the last three months. In fact, yesterday was his third visit. Sorry if I sound a bit like an old biddy peeking round the net curtains, but there's bally little else to do in a place like that, but keep an ear and an eye out for what's going on around one.'

'Don't apologise. If I'd been stuck in there, I'd probably have committed murder by now, and be locked up in Broadmoor, if it still exists. So who was this infrequent but regular visitor of his?'

'One of the nurses said it was his nephew,' replied Hugo, unsuspectingly.

'His *nephew*?' boomed Lady Amanda. 'But he was an only child and he never married. How the hell can a nephew visit him, when he hasn't – sorry, hadn't – any brothers or sisters, or in-laws?'

'I don't know, Manda. I'm only repeating what I was told. Don't shoot the messenger. It was your father who was in partnership with him, back in those antediluvian days. I was still a bit of a stripling, back then.'

'Sorry, Hugo. I just don't understand it. Any other information?'

'Yes. Apparently, this 'nephew' always brought along a hip flask filled with Reggie's favourite cocktail, and they shared it during his visit.'

'Yes!' Lady Amanda was back in booming mode.

'Careful, Manda. You nearly made me spill my tea.'

'Again, sorry, but you've just jogged my memory. So much has happened this afternoon that I just forgot all about it. Look here,' she commanded, scuffling in her capacious handbag and pulling out a cocktail glass, a fine old linen handkerchief a barrier against her leaving any fingerprints on its surface.

'I say, old girl! You haven't taken to drinking during the day have you?' enquired Hugo, aware of her love for cocktails when he had last known her.

'Of course not. I actually went into Reggie's room. That's why I was at that ghastly place. Enid Tweedie told me he was in there, when I went to see her in hospital … But that's a completely different story.

'I went there with the specific goal of visiting him, just for old time's sake, you know. But when I got there, that person on reception told me she'd have to ask Matron first. Well, you know me! I wasn't going to wait to be given permission to visit an old family friend, so I checked his room number with the list pinned on the wall, and toddled down to see him, *sans* permit.'

'But he was dead, Manda.'

'I know that now!' she exclaimed in exasperation. 'But I didn't know it then – just shot into his room before anyone saw me, and there he was, covered from top to toe in a white sheet. It gave me quite a turn, I can tell you.'

'So the cocktail glass is from his room?'

'Bingo, Chummy! There were two glasses on the bedside table, and they looked rather out of place in a joint like that, so I sniffed 'em.'

'Ah, the old Golightly nose! Can identify a cocktail at a hundred paces.'

'That's right! And I got it straight away. The cocktail was a 'Strangeways to Oldham': one measure of dark rum, one measure of gin, half a measure of Rose's Lime Cordial, two measures of mandarin juice, one measure of passion fruit juice and two measures of lemonade,' she informed him crisply.

'But there had been something else in those glasses, too – something nasty. And some of the liquid had been spilled on the carpet, so I got down on all fours like a dog, and sniffed that too.'

'Oh, you didn't, Manda. You're quite shameless, you know.'

'And that's how Matron caught me – on all fours, sniffing the carpet.'

'Whatever did you tell her?' asked Hugo, amused at the turn of this tale.

'I told her I was praying for Reggie's immortal soul, nicked an empty glass, and swiftly made my retreat, because I'd heard your voice. Your room seemed as good a place as any to hide, and I didn't fancy being chased by that old harridan, down the drive, with my proof in my handbag. If I'd hesitated, she might have asked why I had my nose to the carpet, and I'd have had to be very rude to her, and told her I was trying to trace the smell of wee that pervades the home.'

'Proof of what?' asked Hugo, referring back to something Amanda had said, almost in passing.

'Why, proof that Reggie Pagnell was murdered, of course. Don't be so dense, Hugo! She even asked me, when I was arranging your escape, if I'd noticed how many glasses there were on his bedside cabinet, so I told her, of course, that I'd only seen one. Let her look amongst her own staff for the phantom cocktail glass snaffler!'

'That's taking two and two and making five, isn't it?'

'Rot! Reggie's gaga. He gets three visits from a nephew who can't exist. The "nephew" always brings a cocktail for them to share. Reggie dies suddenly, after the third of these visits. I turn up, and smell something suspicious in the glasses. Ergo, he was murdered, but by whom, and why?'

'But both the glasses had something nasty in them, you said.'

'Hence the stain on the floor. He had to pour out two drinks, just like he'd done before, and then, when Reggie had drunk his, he must have poured the other back into this hip flask. Have you ever tried pouring anything into a hip flask without a small funnel? It's impossible not to spill something. Hence the spill on the floor. Hence, murder. QED, Hugo.'

Lady Amanda sat with her arms folded, eyeing her old friend with a mutinous glare. 'Well, Hugo?'

'Actually, I think you might be right, after all you've told me. But what are you going to do about it, eh?'

'You mean, "what are *we* going to do about it", Hugo. Well, firstly, I'm going to ring for Beauchamp, and tell him to put this glass somewhere very safe ... I suppose, actually in my safe would be the best bet.'

'I wondered why you'd been holding it in your hankie

like that. And secondly?'

'That's the bit I don't know yet. I think we'll have to sleep on it, but it'll probably involve going to the police station and seeing if I can get anyone to believe my story.

'And now I believe it is a couple of minutes past the Cocktail Hour, so what can I get you?'

'I haven't the faintest idea. I don't know much about cocktails. You choose!'

'Then we'll have what I consider to be the cocktail of the day. *Beauchamp*! A couple of Strangeways to Oldhams, if you please.'

And thus, Lady Amanda Golightly stumbled into her first ever experience of murder: innocent, guileless, but with the inherited cunning that had kept her family in Belchester Towers for a great many generations.

And she had used the 'm' word: murder. Lady Amanda didn't believe in beating about the bush, as has been mentioned before, and she wasn't going to tolerate murder amongst her friends and acquaintances. That was absolutely beyond the pale!

Although she had been aware of its presence in the trailer at the rear of the Rolls the day before, Lady Amanda was shocked and dismayed, the next morning, to see Hugo shuffling along the corridor propelling a Zimmer frame in front of him, on the way to breakfast.

'I say, old crock. I didn't know you were as bad as that!' she declared, as he finally reached the breakfast room door.

''Fraid so, old stick. Doctor says there's nothing to be done about it, though,' he replied ruefully.

'Who's your doctor?' she asked, abruptly.

'Old Anstruther,' he replied, concentrating on getting his frame over a crack in the flagstones.

'Anstruther? Why, he must have been Methuselah's

doctor! Have you had a second opinion? Been to the hospital for X-rays? Had blood tests?'

'He says there's no point, Manda.'

'No point? The silly old coot. He was practically in his dotage when I was a gal. I'll give my own doctor a ring – sharp young chap, he is – and get you signed on to his books. If there's anything that can be done, he'll not only know about it, but put it into practice. We can't have you trailing round the house like a tortoise, with that thing as your foregoing shell.'

'If you say so, but I can't see him coming up with anything new.'

'Anaesthetics are probably new to that old windbag you've been going to. I'll phone after breakfast and make an appointment for you. In the meantime, we've got to get you mobile, and out in the fresh air for some exercise, to strengthen up those old muscles of yours.

'I know what we'll do,' decided his hostess, as they entered the breakfast room and took their places at the table. 'Did you see my old black trike yesterday?'

'Of course I did. It went in the trailer with my walking frame, when you collected me from the home,' replied Hugo, with some dignity. He was neither blind, nor unobservant.

'Well, that was Mummy's everyday conveyance. For high days and holidays, she had a red one – not quite so heavy, or difficult to steer, and it's in the stables. Also, Daddy used to have a bicycle with a little motor-thingy. If I can get Beauchamp to transfer the motor-thingy from the bicycle to Mummy's red trike – he'll work something out to take into account the extra wheel – we can go out for picnics, even if we never get out of the grounds.'

'That sounds jolly pleasant, Manda,' he replied, his good humour restored, at the thought of outings and outside – two things he'd been severely deprived of, of late.

21

Beauchamp laid out a dish of fried kippers on the table, and as Hugo was starting to enquire about what they would do with regard to their suspicions of murder, Lady Amanda upbraided him with, 'You know one never discusses business at table, Hugo. We'll talk about it after we've eaten. While we're at breakfast, tell me about your extraordinarily long surname, and how it grew that big. I never have known the full story.'

'Oh, that's an easy one,' he began, interspersing the tale with breaks, while he forked mouthfuls of kipper from his plate, and chewed them appreciatively. 'Two strong women were all it took. Grandpa Cholmondley married a Miss Crichton and, anxious that her name should not be discarded so lightly, she insisted on adding it to his, making it double-barrelled.

'My father, in his choice of bride, married an equally strong woman, but with the unfortunate surname of Crump. Well, she prevailed, probably egged on by, and in the same fashion as, her mother-in-law, and the name became triple-barrelled, as you now know it.'

'But you never married, Hugo?'

'Didn't dare to, in case I chose a similarly strong-minded bride. Might have ended up with a moniker so long, I'd never be able to fill in a form for the rest of my life. It's bad enough as it is, without making it even longer. Pen keeps running out of ink, don't yer know.'

'Don't be flippant, Chummy. Is that the real reason you never married?'

'Of course it's not. Just never met the right gal, I suppose.'

'Never mind. We can keep each other company now, can't we?'

'I was going to ask you about that,' Hugo replied. 'Didn't know if it was quite decent, the two of us living under the same roof, and all that. It's all been a bit sudden. I'll understand completely, if you think you acted rather rashly, yesterday.'

'Don't be absurd!' she spluttered, her mouth full of tea. 'I'm glad of the company, to be quite honest, and we have known each other for a very long time.'

'But with an exceedingly long gap in between.'

'Certainly! But we're still the same people, aren't we? I know I haven't changed my nature very much, and from what I've seen, neither have you. Now look here, Hugo: we can be lonely separately, or we can choose to be in company together. Which is the most attractive option to you? I know which I'd choose, and I have. When one is older, sometimes the luxury of one's pride and independence is something one shouldn't even attempt to pay for. Do you want to go back to that dreadful home?'

'No,' agreed Hugo, and addressed himself to a clean plate, for toast and marmalade. 'Do you remember how I used to carry you around on my shoulders, when you were still quite a tot?'

'Of course I do,' she replied. 'I sometimes wonder if it was that lofty view that made me a bit haughty at times. One never knows, does one?'

A little later, as Beauchamp cleared away the breakfast things, Lady Amanda decided to make some telephone calls, and, spotting Hugo over by the window, she called over to him, 'Do you think you could get me my little address book? It's on the whatnot.'

Looking round quizzically, Hugo enquired mildly, 'What whatnot?'

'The window whatnot,'

'What's on the window whatnot?'

'I'll get it myself. If we go on like this, we're going to slide into the "Who's on next?" sketch that Abbot and Costello did.'

'What?' asked Hugo.

'Never mind! I just want to make a few calls, then ring for an appointment for you with my doctor, and check out a couple of estate agents about getting tenants for your house. And you can ring up the one who's trying to sell it, and tell him to take it off the market. Then, we've got to work out what to do about the "you-know-what".'

'What "you-know-what"? Is the "you-know-what" on the window whatnot, or what?' Hugo replied, nearly restarting the surreal conversation that Lady Amanda had just forcibly ended, before it got out of control, and drove her mad.

Chapter Three

After a very intense hour on the phone, Lady Amanda was as good as her word earlier, and instructed Beauchamp on the alterations she required, with the motor from the bicycle being suitably adapted and transferred to Mummy's best red trike, then mounted her own machine, having decided that she owed it to the police, to give them a crack at solving this case of murder she and Hugo had uncovered.

She arrived in South Street in Belchester, where the police station was situated, just beyond The Goat and Compasses public house. Leaving her tricycle firmly chained up, she went through the police station doors and presented herself at the desk, where a fresh-faced uniformed officer sat, reading the sports pages of a daily paper that she would never allow to darken the letter box of her own home.

'Can I help you, madam?' he asked, pushing the newspaper aside and looking up, his facial expression freezing a little, as he noticed that she was neither young, nor pretty.

'I sincerely hope so, young man,' she replied, thinking that he looked no older than a schoolboy. Wherever were the police recruiting from nowadays? It'd be from the nursery next. 'I wish to report a murder,' she stated baldly, and watched his face change from slight disappointment, to 'we've got a right one, here'.

'How can I help you with this "murder", madam?' he asked politely, the word murder obviously carrying inverted commas, and with a sarcastic gleam in his eye.

'I'd like to speak to the officer in charge, if you don't mind. Murder is a serious matter, and should be treated as such, don't you think?'

'Of course, madam. I'll ring upstairs for the inspector, if you'll be so good as to wait here.'

Lady Amanda took a seat on a hard wooden bench on the wall opposite the desk, but her hearing was still acute, and she heard the young man's end of the conversation without any difficulty. 'Got a right one down here. Some batty old biddy wanting to report a murder. Wants to see someone in charge. Do you think you could have a word with her?'

The answer must have been in the affirmative, for he proceeded to conduct her up a flight of stairs and into a small, unaired office that smelled of sweat and 'fags smoked out of the window'.

In five minutes, she found herself back outside once more, feeling both silly, and furious at the same time; silly, because the inspector – too young for his rank, in her opinion – had treated her as if she were senile, and furious, because she had let him get away with it, which wasn't like her at all. She hadn't had much to do with the police, in her time, however, and it could have been that which threw her so far out of her normal commanding and forthright character.

More likely, however, it was the insolent and superior attitude of the inspector, who had asked her if she thought she was some sort of 'Miss Marple' character, and enquiring if she watched a lot of detective programmes on what he had referred to as 'the telly'. She had retorted with as much dignity as she could muster, by informing him that: A) Miss Marple was a fictional character, B) Miss Marple was portrayed as a very elderly lady, and C), Miss Marple managed to traverse the decades without ageing a day, and that, as she was none of these three things, she certainly did not see herself in such a role; and she marched out of the police station in high dudgeon.

So, that was that! The police were going to take no notice of her whatsoever. Granted, she hadn't brought the cocktail glass with her, but they'd probably just have taken it, washed it up, and put it away behind the police social club bar.

So, she'd hang on to it. And she and Hugo would find out who killed poor old Reggie Pagnell themselves.

She rode back to Belchester Towers via the back routes, taking her time, to allow her temper to subside, and to try to come to terms with the fact that the police thought her a silly old fool. As she entered the grounds, she looked across to the building where she had spent her entire life (when not at boarding school).

There it stood, its red brick dulled by age now, though it was less than two hundred years old, with its silly moat empty, overgrown by weeds. There it stood, with its daft towers, and all its unrealistic fairy-tale architecture, and she loved it. Tears came to her eyes as she thought of all the happy times she had spent there throughout her life, accompanied by tears of self-pity, at how she had been treated at the police station.

Well, she had Hugo for company now, and they'd show that snotty inspector how to track down a murderer, and then who would be laughing? Eh?

When she had parked her trike, she went into the morning room and encountered Hugo taking a leisurely look at the newspaper. Looking up, he was immediately aware that Manda was not herself – something had happened that had 'got to her'. 'What's up, old thing?' he asked, in a gentle voice.

'Oh, nothing, Chummy. I've just discovered that when one is old, nobody notices one, or listens to one any more. The elderly become invisible, and I feel that, today, I have

27

joined their silent and unnoticed ranks.'

'Rot, Manda! You? Old? Utter and complete tommyrot!'

'Very gallant of you, Hugo, but I have to face the fact that I'm just a meddling old woman in most people's eyes.'

'What's happened to make you feel like that?' asked Hugo, with concern. This wasn't the Manda that he remembered and … was – well – very fond of, at least.

'I went to the police station to report Reggie Pagnell's murder, and was treated as a silly old trout with an over-active imagination,' she informed him, looking thoroughly crestfallen.

'How dare they! We must speak to the Chief Constable, now. That really takes the biscuit!' Hugo retorted, now full of indignation.

'Times have moved on, since we were in our prime, Hugo. The Chief Constable's a young man in his mid-forties, I believe, and although Daddy knew his father, I predict that if we put our little problem before him, he'd just think it was dementia setting in, as so many people now presume, about anything esoteric, said by someone over pensionable age.'

'Then we'll just have to investigate it ourselves. Can't have a murderer wandering about out there, scot free and undetected.'

'I hoped you'd say that, Hugo. That's what I'd more or less decided myself, on the way home. I just didn't know if you'd go along with it or not. I'll start with the nursing home: see what details I can get about this "nephew", and about when and where the funeral's to be held.'

'That's more like my Manda of old. Up and at 'em! Don't let 'em grind you down! When are you thinking of going?'

'After luncheon,' she replied, tugging on a chintz bell-pull to summon Beauchamp, and announce that they were ready for their meal.

Unnervingly, Beauchamp slipped through the door the moment she grabbed the bell-pull, and she gave a little shriek, at this immediate attendance upon her wishes. 'I wish you wouldn't do that, Beauchamp. At least give a little cough, to warn me you're just about to appear, like a pantomime villain, as usual.'

'Sorry, my lady. And it's Beecham,' the man declared, his dignity not ruffled one jot.

'Tell me, did you study French at school, *Beauchamp*?' she asked, emphasising the pronunciation of his surname.

'No, my lady. I studied woodwork. But it's still Beecham.' And with that, he disappeared out of the room, to bring the food to table in the breakfast room, where it was cosier to eat, at this time of day, than in the vast panelled dining room.

Over their meal, the proposed investigation banned until after they had finished eating, the conversation was of a nostalgic nature – not unexpectedly, given the circumstances that had suddenly thrown them together again, after such a long time.

'Nice name that – Amanda,' Hugo mumbled through a mouthful of food. 'Lady Amanda, now that's just the same as the woman in those Campion books by whatshername – Margery Allingham. That's the chap. Lady Amanda Fitton, wasn't it? Did you ever read those books, Manda?' he asked.

'Actually, Mummy named me after her. The writer only had the copyright on the books, you know, not the characters' names as well. But Mummy loved all those old murder mysteries, and I read them when I was growing up. Used to imagine it was me, marrying silly young Albert. And here I am, never managed to find Mr Right, or even Mr Wright – that's with a 'W', Hugo, as one can't hear spelling. Joke!'

'Jolly good! Play on words. I seem to remember you

were rather good at those, when we were younger, but that one definitely needs to be written down to appreciate it.'

After a few seconds of silence, Hugo declared, 'Damn shame, you being orphaned like that!'

'Damned lucky escape, if you ask me!'

'Whatever do you mean, Manda? That sounds rather cruel, and that's unlike you.'

'It's just sheer logic, old bean. The only people who never have to face up to the loss of their parents, are those who die young, and I never had any intentions of doing that.'

'Ah, see what you mean. True enough! You always were a sensible old thing.'

'And not so much of the "old". I've had a bellyful of that today already, and you're a good few years my senior, if my memory really isn't failing.'

'Touché!'

'Oh, by the way, Beauchamp has transferred that motor thingy from Daddy's bicycle to mother's best tricycle, so we can get out and about.'

'Bravo, Beauchamp!' Hugo replied, waving his fork about, in his excitement. 'We could be like those Hell's Angels chappies, what?'

'More like Hell's Wrinklies! And mind your fork! You nearly chucked your food on the floor, waving it about like that.'

'Sorry, Manda.'

After coffee and a suitable period for digestion, Lady Amanda mounted her three-wheeled steed and set off to see what she could learn from the rest home where she had discovered Hugo incarcerated, the day before.

She had a legitimate family reason for knowing when, and where, Reggie's funeral would take place, and the same thing applied to getting in touch with his so-called nephew, to pass on her condolences. She'd present a humbler version of herself today, and explain away her behaviour of the day before as shock, pure and simple.

If anyone made a fuss about her 'kidnapping' of Hugo, she would say that had also been due to the shock of Reggie's demise, and stumbling upon her old friend, after so long a time. She could certainly tell them that he was happy and settled, and that they needn't bother themselves about his welfare any more. He would be more than adequately cared for at Belchester Towers. Maybe the address would impress them. Maybe her own name would, too, for she didn't remember formally introducing herself on her last visit, and thought that remedying that might improve their treatment of her no end.

She duly parked her trike and chained it to a sturdy chain-link fence and then entered, her hopes of success high. The woman on duty at reception was the same one as the day before and, on seeing Lady Amanda approach her for the second time in two days, cringed, and put her hand under the desk, presumably to ring a panic bell.

'Good afternoon, young lady,' cooed Lady Amanda, holding out her hand in greeting. 'I'd like to apologise for my rather excitable behaviour yesterday, and introduce myself properly. I am Lady Amanda Golightly of Belchester Towers.'

That seemed to have done the trick, and by the time that Matron arrived at the double, prepared for anything, after the panic bell having been used, she surveyed the figure of Lady Amanda, and inhaled hugely, to give her a piece of her mind.

It was only the immediate intervention of the receptionist that deflated her bubble. 'This is Lady Amanda Golightly of Belchester Towers,' the woman informed the purple-faced tyrant, 'and she's come to apologise for yesterday. Shock, you know, at finding one old friend dead, and another resident here.'

That was Matron efficiently torpedoed, and the sour-

31

faced woman had to force a smile on to her disapproving countenance. 'So pleased to be introduced to you at last, my lady,' she dripped, shaking hands with a hand like a wet fish. 'What can we do for you today? Let you remove another resident or two? Why not the whole lot, then you can have a very jolly time at The Towers.

Hmph! The woman wasn't quite dead in the water yet, thought Lady Amanda. She'd have to continue with the charm offensive. 'Apart from apologise, all I wanted was to get details of poor old Reggie Pagnell's funeral, and maybe his nephew's address, so that I could convey my condolences on the loss of his uncle.' She sounded almost like Mary Poppins, so anxious was she to get her hands on the information she needed to start the investigation.

But Matron wasn't giving in that easily. It took more than Lady Amanda on her best behaviour to make her crumble and fly the white flag. 'I'm afraid we're not permitted to give out personal information about our "guests",' she intoned, a wolf-like smile shaping her lips. 'However …' Here, she held up a hand, to stem the flow that was preparing itself to fall from Lady Amanda's sneering mouth.

'However,' she repeated, 'we can provide you with the name of Mr Pagnell's solicitor, who will provide you with any information he deems necessary, in the circumstances.'

'Thank you so much.' Lady Amanda was back in purring mode. The solicitor's address would probably net her more than she was ever likely to get from this old harridan, and if she needed any inside knowledge about Reggie's residence here, Enid Tweedie could prove to be just the right cat's paw to get her insider information.

If Lady Amanda footed the bill, she was sure Enid would not be averse to a few days – a week at the most – convalescing here, and being her 'agent' on the inside. It would also give her another excuse to be here on the premises, as she still might need to return.

Clutching the piece of paper with the name 'Freeman, Hardy, Williams and Williams' and an address in East Street in her hand, she walked thoughtfully out to her trike, placed the piece of paper carefully in her handbag, put it in the front basket of the vehicle, and made her way back to Belchester Towers, determined to make a proper appointment to visit Reggie's solicitor. She'd almost suspected the name of the law firm to be fictitious, when she had first learnt it. 'Sounds just like a shoe shop we used to have in the town,' she'd muttered under her breath, when she'd read it, but it obviously wasn't.

But she must make a good fist of this next part of the exercise. It wouldn't do to 'blow it', as she had done at the nursing home. Advance warning of who she was might make all the difference to how they treated her at the law firm, and she didn't want just to blunder in and make the wrong impression. She'd already done that at the police station, and look where that had got her – playing at sleuth, actually!

She'd have to get her violin out when she got home. Oh, and have a rummage around for Daddy's old deerstalker. (Lady Amanda had undertaken tuition, in her schooldays, in playing the violin, flute and piano, and had, of course, excelled at all three!)

Back at Belchester Towers, she dug her violin out of the lumber room, where it had slumbered for many a year, and shoved some old sheet music on to the lectern in the library, to have a good old play. She was only halfway through the 'March' from *Scipio* (for the third time) when Hugo shuffled through the door, propelling his walking frame before him.

'What's that dreadful racket? Thought someone was torturing a cat in here, so I came to investigate,' he asked, closing the door behind him, lest Beauchamp should become aware of the fearful row, and poke his nose in.

'Bit out of practice,' Lady Amanda excused herself. 'Couldn't find you when I got home, so I thought I'd look out the jolly old fiddle – Sherlock Holmes, and all that. See if it put me in the right frame of mind for this sleuthing we've decided to take on.'

'I was having a little nap,' explained Hugo, looking slightly embarrassed. 'Food makes me feel rather like a snake after a large feed. I just want to curl up somewhere and snooze.'

'No need to make excuses to me, Hugo. We are the age that we are, and we must just live with that. The alternative's unthinkable. And we must, therefore, ensure that we don't indulge in too large a feast before we have to go out investigating. Wouldn't want to be caught asleep on the job, would we?'

'I should hope not. What's the next move then?' asked Hugo eagerly.

'I've made an appointment with Reggie's solicitor for tomorrow morning. I couldn't get a thing out of that mato at the nursing home, except for the name of his legal representative, so I thought I'd go and beard him in his den, so to speak.'

'Jolly good idea. You will be gentle with him though, won't you, Manda?'

'Gentle? I'll charm his socks off. You might not know it, but I can be darned persuasive, when I want to be.'

'I don't doubt that for one moment. So, what happens now, or is that it, for today?' enquired Hugo, wondering if he might not be able to slip off to continue his forty winks.

'We're going outside so that you can test-drive your new mode of transport. I told you Beauchamp had finished the job. Now we need to see how you get on with the thing.'

'What, right now?' asked the elderly Hugo, disappointed that yet more action was called for.

'Yes. Right now! You know there's no such thing as a dull moment with me, old stick,' she declared.

'No such thing as a peaceful one either, if I remember correctly,' mumbled Hugo, but he did it very quietly, not wanting to hurt her feelings, after she'd been so kind as to take him under her wing like this, and rescue him from that living grave he had been existing in before.

His spirits raised considerably, though, when she announced that it was much later than she had thought, and that it was, once more, cocktail time, and that they must hurry inside, so as not to miss a moment of it. She had earlier instructed Beauchamp, to set out two of the 'cocktails of the moment' in the drawing room, and they should be waiting for them now, icy cold and deliciously relaxing.

Chapter Four

The next morning, after breakfast, Lady Amanda requested that Beauchamp give the Rolls a bit more of a buff-up than it had needed to collect Hugo, and meet her outside the front entrance (a proper road-crossing having been provided, many years ago, over the old moat) at ten-thirty sharp. 'Oh, and wear your chauffeur's livery,' she commanded him.

'One wants to make a good impression,' she informed her ever-patient employee, 'and you always looked so amusing in that cap.' This addition rather spoiled what had sounded very much like a compliment, but Beauchamp took it all in his stride, as he did Lady Amanda's many strange ways and eccentricities, and was ready and waiting in the car, at two minutes before the half hour.

Lady Amanda emerged as the stable clock was chiming, dressed very smartly in a silk summer suit and her best hat. (Blimey! thought Beauchamp. She *is* going to town.) Entering the car and settling herself comfortably, she blew through the speaking tube to get his attention. 'Yes, my lady?' he replied, sliding open the window between the back and the front of the car.

'Oh, do use the tube, Beauchamp. It's so much more fun if you use the tube,' she implored him.

'Yes, my lady. If you say so, my lady, but I can't understand a word you're saying when we use the tube. You'll just have to tell me through this here window, and then pretend that we did it down the tube,' he advised.

'Very well, but you're a spoilsport and a party-pooper, Beauchamp!' she retorted.

'That's Beecham, my lady!' he replied, but he said it down the tube, so that she wouldn't be able to decipher what he'd said.

'Take me to East Street. I have an appointment at Freeman, Hardy, Williams and Williams at eleven o'clock, and I don't want to be late.'

Half an hour may seem a long time, for a journey of a little more than a mile and a half, but in the ancient Rolls-Royce, it would take them all of that time to achieve their goal, and both of them understood that. The ancient vehicle shuddered to a start, and Lady Amanda set off on the next stage of her adventure.

The receptionist at the legal firm informed her that her appointment was with *young* Mr Williams, so she was therefore very surprised when an ancient man with two walking sticks and only a few wisps of white hair, beckoned her into an office opposite the reception desk.

'Do take a seat, Mrs ah – Mrs um …' he quavered, creaking slowly down into the seat behind the desk; a large padded leather seat that dwarfed him, and made him look like an elderly child.

'Lady Amanda Golightly,' his client trilled, on her very best behaviour.

'Speak up, Mrs – Mrs?' young Mr Williams spake.

'Lady Amanda Golightly,' she almost shouted, and that seemed to do the trick, for he nodded his head very slowly, and muttered, 'Belchester Towers! Well, well, well!'

'That's right, Mr Williams, and I'm here to see you about the death of a very old family friend who has just passed away. Mr Reginald Pagnell.' She hated euphemisms, but she could hardly have told him that Reggie had been murdered. She was on her best behaviour, and must not stray from the path.

She was glad she was not consulting the old boy on anything confidential, for she knew that, at this volume, everything she said would be clearly audible in the reception area, and probably in the adjacent rooms as well.

'Mr Pagnell? Pagnell?' There was a pause, as the little gnome of a man gathered his woolly thoughts together. 'Ah, yes, Pagnell! What can I do for you in respect of the late Mr Pagnell, dear lady?'

'I'm trying to find his "nephew",' she could not help herself uttering this last word in a voice clearly indicating disbelief in the existence of such a person. 'Apparently he had got into the habit of visiting his uncle once a month, at the nursing home, where he was residing. I should like to speak to him about his uncle, whom I had not seen for a number of years, just for old times' sake.'

'A nephew? Nephew? Can't recall any nephew, dear lady. I shall just call for a little assistance, and maybe Carole in reception can have a look in the records.' Thus saying, he picked up the internal telephone, of which he had no real need, considering the volume to which his own voice had risen, so that he could hear himself speak, and asked if the receptionist could have a quick scan of their records, in search of a nephew for Mr Reginald Pagnell (deceased).

The answer came almost immediately, that they had no record of any living relatives for their late client, the last one being a cousin who had died some five years ago.

Having received this unhelpful information, Lady Amanda tried another tack. 'Would it be possible to know the terms of Mr Pagnell's will?' she asked, in as charming a voice as she could muster, given the decibels at which this request had to be made.

'Hoping to be remembered, are we?' shouted the old man, with a wheezy chuckle.

'No, no, nothing like that, I assure you, Mr Williams. I'd just like to know, for the sake of personal interest,' she cooed, like a pigeon using a megaphone.

'Can't just give out confidential information like that,

dear lady. I'm sure you understand,' Mr Williams countered.

'But the will will be read soon, and then it will be published, and in the public domain,' she pleaded.

'Have to wait a bit then, won't you,' the old solicitor informed her, a wicked twinkle in his eye, at having thus thwarted her.

Gathering her considerable resolve together, Lady Amanda made one last thrust. 'Can you give me the details of the funeral, then – time, place?' She almost, but not quite, begged him.

At the mention of the word 'funeral', the old man drifted off in to a brown study, and began muttering: quite loudly as it happens, but because of his deafness, clearly audible to Lady Amanda.

'Queer thing, that, about the funeral. Mr Pagnell left clear instructions that he was to be interred in the family plot, in the churchyard of St Michael-in-the-Fields. Sole beneficiary, after a number of small bequests, or rather his representative, has been pestering to have the old boy cremated. Don't fancy that, myself. Want my skull and cross-bones all together, when the Last Trump sounds.'

Now, looking up at his client once more, he continued, as if he had intended her to hear what he had been saying to himself all along, 'Absolutely impossible in the light of my late client's wishes. Cremation, my gouty old foot! He shall be interred where he requested to be interred.

'That was his last wish, and it is my job to make sure that that is how things happen. St Michael-in-the-Fields, next Wednesday at ten-thirty, then afterwards, at the deceased's old address, High Hedges, The Butts, Belchester. I think that is all the information I can give you, but it has been arranged that the will-reading take place after the wake. Perhaps you might find yourself there at the appropriate time, young lady. I shall certainly not object to your presence,' young Mr Williams concluded, constructing on his crumpled old face what Lady Amanda correctly construed to be a conspiratorial smile.

'Is there any information you can give me as to the identity of the sole beneficiary?' she asked, hopefully.

'Sorry, young lady, but you will just have to be patient, and all will be revealed.'

She blushed with pleasure to have been addressed as 'young lady', not just once, but twice, and made her farewells suitably appreciatively, if a little on the *fortissimo* side.

As she re-entered the Rolls, she mused on what she had learnt. Next Wednesday; and it was Friday today, so she and Hugo had five days to determine whether they were capable of discovering the identity of the young man who had visited the nursing home, with such deadly refreshment about his person.

On arrival back at Belchester Towers, she shared what little she had learnt with Hugo.

'Well, that seems to be that then, old thing,' he commented when she had made her little speech. 'Nothing we can do now, but wait.'

'Rot, Hugo! There's plenty to be done.'

'Well, I can't see it.'

'No, but, luckily, I can. And don't you find it very suspicious that that "nephew" of Reggie's – because that's who this mysterious representative of his beneficiary is – has kept banging on about cremating his "uncle", when it was strictly against Reggie's dying wish? I do, and it sounds like he's trying to prevent the opportunity for an exhumation, should anyone suspect him of poisoning his "uncle".

'So, the first thing I'm going to do is phone the hospital and find out when Enid Tweedie is going to be discharged. Then I'm going to visit that ghastly nursing home again, and book her in for a week's convalescence.'

'I say, that's a bit mean, isn't it?'

'Not at all,' retorted Lady Amanda. 'She'll be an undercover agent, for us.'

'Oh, I see what you mean,' said Hugo, nodding his head of thick, wavy white hair.

'And anyway, I'll be paying, so she can hardly complain, can she?'

This was a rhetorical question, and was recognised as such by Hugo, so he just kept his mouth shut, and waited to hear what other plans she had made. 'On my third visit to the nursing home,' she commenced, spearing him with a gimlet-eyed glance, 'I shall ask to see the rooms they use for short-term convalescent patients.

'It said on their sign outside that they also offer convalescent and respite care, and I shall be perfectly within my rights, as I intend to send some business their way, much as I abhor the idea, but Tweedie's a tough cookie. She has to be, as when she's fit, and up and about, she comes in here once a week to 'do the rough', and she's got a real horror of a mother living with her, too. She'll cope. She'll be glad of the break.

'What I can't ferret out on my visit, I can leave it to her to do, chatting to the staff, and drawing them out. She can pretend to have been old Reggie's cleaner at some time, and improvise some reminiscences, to allay any fears her prey may have.'

'Top hole, Manda!' cheered Hugo, amazed at the tenacity and inventiveness of his old friend. 'Then what?'

'If we still haven't got our bird, going to the funeral and the wake should give us more idea of the identity of this mystery beneficiary, and we just take it from there. I refuse to go back to the police again, until I have the murdering beggar bang to rights, and can have him charged for the dog he is. That'll show that uppity, disrespectful inspector a thing or two!'

'Don't turn this into a personal crusade, Manda,' Hugo

implored her, knowing what she could be like.

'It IS personal. Daddy and Reggie were partners, back when they were young. Reggie dissolved the partnership and moved away to do something else, but he obviously returned to the town of his birth, when he retired. I remember him from when I was a tot, and I'm not going to let a personable man like that get himself murdered, and no one be any the wiser.

'Whoever shortened his life by even a day is going to pay for that theft of time, and do some time of his own. Hmph!' she concluded, a determined expression on her face. 'Let's see, today's Friday, so tomorrow's Saturday. I'll go to the nursing home tomorrow, when they should be swamped with visitors who usually work during the week, so they'll be busy, and not so "on their guard".

'But, now, to more practical matters. There is a very elderly lift in this building, which was put in for Grandmama, who needed to use a wheelchair. I'll get Beauchamp to oil the thing up, and get it into working order. That way, you'll be able to explore a bit more of the house, if you get bored.

'I've also noticed that you have some trouble with your walker thingy, getting up and down the steps in the corridors, where the floor levels change. No, Hugo! Let me finish! We used to have dachshunds, and when there was a litter, the pups' legs were so short that they couldn't get round the place very easily, so we put ramps at all the steps.

'BEAUCHAMP!' Here, she broke off to give an ear-splitting yell, and Hugo winced at the assault upon his ears. 'I'll get Beauchamp to get them out of the attics and put them in place again. That will make life much easier for you, getting around.

'And, by the way, you have an appointment with my GP tonight, at five-thirty, to see about those worn-out old pins of yours. I shall, of course, accompany you, and

Beauchamp can take us there in the Rolls. Argh!' she suddenly screamed, for Beauchamp had just appeared at her shoulder. She hadn't even noticed him entering the room.

'Dammit, Beauchamp, I'm sure you're not human. There's something of the supernatural about you that just can't be explained.'

'That's Beecham, my lady,' intoned Beauchamp, in a bored monotone.

While Beauchamp went about his business as instructed by his employer, Lady Amanda escorted Hugo outside, to have his first lesson in riding a motorised tricycle. He was rather averse to the idea, himself, but she insisted, and even fetched his walking frame for him.

'You just wait outside, and I'll ride them both round to the front. Then I'll show you how to control the motorised one – once I've worked it out for myself – and you can have a go, yourself' she informed him.

'I'd rather not, Manda. The whole idea terrifies me.'

'Stuff and nonsense! It's no different to driving round in one of those motorised shopping thingies that so many old people seem to have. It's just cheaper, that's all – recycling, in its best form. Recycling! Haha! Good one, don't you think? Maybe I should have said "re-tricycling"?' She went off into peals of delighted laughter, at her own accidental joke.

Recognising a lost cause when he saw one, Hugo gave in, with as good a grace as he could muster, considering how apprehensive he felt.

Lady Amanda disappeared off to the stables and, in due course, appeared again, pedalling the black tricycle that she used almost on a daily basis. She then trotted off once more, there was a muted roar, as of a motor being over-revved, and, amid a cloud of black smoke, an apparition appeared, rounding the corner of the house, emitting loud hooting noises of despair, and Lady Amanda shot past him, managing to stop, just short of the moat.

As the smoke began to clear, Hugo could make out her figure more clearly, pushing the ancient velocipede towards him, the engine not engaged. 'Bit trickier than I thought,' she puffed, as she drew up alongside him. 'I'll have to get Beauchamp to work out how best to handle it, and then we'll try again. No point in going off at half cock, is there, Hugo, old bean?'

'Absolutely none, Manda,' agreed Hugo, with great relief. He would be spared the indignity of making a fool of himself, for today at least, and would do his best to discourage her from trying again in the near future.

'Best go in and have a little lie-down, I think. Then we can think of afternoon tea, and getting ready to drag you off to the quack's – get something positive done to make you a bit more mobile.

'His name's Dr Andrew: Campbell Andrew, and he's a very helpful and obliging young chap, so listen to what he says, and no arguments. Agreed, Hugo?'

'No, ma'am,' replied Hugo a trifle testily. He knew perfectly well how to behave towards doctors: he'd seen enough of old Anstruther in the last couple of years to last him a lifetime, and he'd never uttered a discourteous word to the old man, no matter how cross or disappointed he was at his diagnoses.

They were sitting in the surgery's waiting room, keeping an eye on the red light above the door of the doctor's consulting room. The receptionist had informed them that they were after the old lady with the shopping trolley, and she was in there at the moment. They would not see her leave, as a door from the consulting room let patients debouch into another corridor, but once the red light turned green, they could go in.

With a buzz, the red light abruptly changed its colour,

and they were off, Lady Amanda knocking on the door, Hugo following slowly behind with his walking frame. He had a feeling he would not have much contribution to make in the ensuing consultation, and he just wanted to get it over and done with.

Dr Andrew turned out to be a man in his early forties, still with a full head of hair, and a kindly face, and after greeting them both, he bade them take a seat. Having waited for Hugo to get comfortable, Lady Amanda rather thoughtlessly, in Hugo's opinion, opened the proceedings, and immediately ordered him to stand up and walk about, so that the doctor could see how bad his problem was.

'Come along, Hugo! Right turn, and walk! Left turn, and walk! Sit! Rise! Atten-shun! Stand at *ease*!' she barked, like an RSM.

'I think that's enough for now. He's not on parade, or at Crufts,' said Dr Andrew, and thoughtfully came round to the other side of the desk to feel over Hugo's worn-out joints, not making him climb up on to the couch usually used for such examinations.

'Had any X-rays done by your last GP?' he asked, and was flabbergasted when Hugo replied in the negative.

'Who was your last GP?' he then asked.

'Dr Anstruther,' replied Hugo, feeling slightly flustered at what he felt was a defection.

'Ah!' Doctor Andrew needed to say no more, and Lady Amanda just snorted.

'I'll just ring the hospital now, and make you an appointment to see a specialist – get you in to see him as soon as possible. Can't have you tottering around like that, if there's something simple that will remedy it,' Dr Andrew explained, as he waited for his call to be answered.

'Ah, hello there. Dr Andrew from the Summerfield Road practice. Could I have a quick word with Dr Updyke, please? It is rather urgent.' As he waited for his call to be put through, he smiled reassuringly across his desk. 'Cedric and I go back a long way,' he informed them – a clue that he might be able to massage the length of the queue to see this particular specialist, through a bit of 'knowing the right person'.

The call was obviously picked up at the other end, for he bent his attention to the receiver again, and began, 'Hello, Cedric. Got a rather interesting case of advanced arthritis here – hips and knees. Not had any prior treatment at all, not even X-rayed as yet. Dr Anstruther. Nuff said. I wondered if you could fit him in at all, urgently.' He paused, then continued, 'A Mr Hugo Cholmondley-Crichton-Crump – an old friend of Lady Amanda Golightly,' he added, for the sake of Lady Amanda's pride.

There was an irate squawking noise from the other end of the telephone, which took Dr Andrew a couple of minutes to quell. 'How terribly unfortunate, but I'd rather you didn't let that colour your judgement, of course. This is really of the utmost urgency, in my opinion.' He was silent for another minute and a half, then made his good-byes, and ended the call.

'Monday at nine thirty a.m., Mr Cholmondley-Crichton-Crump. Dr Cedric Updyke, at the main hospital.' He then turned his attention to Lady Amanda, and speared her with his eye. 'Who's been a naughty girl then?' he asked, fighting a grin.

'What have I done now?' Lady Amanda asked in puzzlement, unable to understand why attention should suddenly have turned to her, when the phone call had been about Hugo.

'I hear you've been riding that trike of yours at high speed, without due care and attention, and have been involved in a hit-and-run, the scene of which you left, without reporting the matter,' he explained.

Lady Amanda blushed, as she remembered the man

who had had to dive for safety, as her trike had careered down the hospital drive. 'I say, it wasn't *him*, was it?' she asked, now thoroughly embarrassed.

'It was! And I understand that you've been fined for speeding,' Dr Andrew added, no longer able to suppress his amusement.

'Stuff and nonsense,' she blustered. 'He shouldn't have got in my way.'

'Well, you're lucky, in a way, that he did. The thought of you taking another crack at him got him thoroughly rattled, and that's why Mr Cholmondley-Crichton-Crump's appointment is so soon. He assumes that you will arrive in a more orthodox vehicle, given your friend's condition, and he said that if he could get it over with as soon as possible, it would save him getting paranoid every time he has to walk down or cross the entrance road.'

'Oh, we will, we will,' Lady Amanda assured him. 'We'll get Beauchamp to bring us in the Rolls,' she said, with relief.

'Good! And I'm sure we can improve the quality of your life, with all the modern techniques we have these days,' he assured Hugo. 'Soon have you up and about, and getting about, with a lot more ease. I can't promise you that you'll ever get back on a tennis court, for we can do nothing about reaction time, but I'm sure we can get you walking with minimum discomfort, and maybe indulging in a bit of dancing – just for exercise, and to strengthen the muscles,' he reassured a rather alarmed Hugo. He'd never liked tennis, but wasn't completely averse to a slow waltz or two.

'Thank you very much indeed, Doctor. It's very good of you to take the time like this,' he spluttered, unable to believe that his pain and struggle for mobility might soon be things of the past.

'No trouble, Mr – uh, may I call you Hugo? Just to save time, you understand. Your surnames are a bit of a mouthful, I'm afraid.'

'No problem, Doctor. And thank you, once more, from the bottom of my heart.'

'I think you ought to thank Lady Amanda as well. If she hadn't nearly run over Dr Updyke, and frightened the life out of him, he'd never have agreed to see you so promptly.'

'Marvellous!' exclaimed Hugo, accepting the walking frame offered to him by Lady Amanda, and they exited the consulting room, well-satisfied with the visit.

Back at The Towers once more, and seated in the drawing room, Lady Amanda hardly had time to consult her watch, before Beauchamp entered, silently as ever, bearing a silver salver which held two cocktail glasses, filled to the brim. 'Your drinks, my lady,' he intoned, and put them down on a small side table. 'Strangeways to Oldham,' he informed them, before slipping away as noiselessly as a cat.

Chapter Five

The next morning, armed with the knowledge that Enid Tweedie would be discharged on Monday afternoon, Lady Amanda set out early – a passenger once more, in the Rolls – to visit the Birdlings Serenade prison camp, to make enquiries about that lady's convalescence.

Monday was scheduled to be a very busy day, what with Hugo's visit to the orthopaedic consultant, and Enid needing to be transferred from hospital to care home, and then they had the funeral on Wednesday. Life suddenly seemed a lot busier than it used to, she was happy to note, for it was now much more interesting as well.

On arrival at the home, the receptionist recognised her, this time without feeling the need to press the panic button. Lady Amanda's civilised persona, on her last visit, to make enquiries about one of their late clients, had reassured her that she wasn't an escaped lunatic, but a member of the aristocracy, and she greeted the stout figure with a smile.

'Lady Amanda Golightly,' Lady Amanda introduced herself, in case the woman's memory wasn't up to it. 'I understand that you provide convalescent care, as well as full-time,' she stated, hoping for confirmation that this service was still available.

'Of course, your ladyship,' replied the woman, with the slight bob of a curtsey, which she could do nothing to avoid. Her legs just responded to the title automatically. 'We always keep a couple of rooms free for people who wish to convalesce with us, or for relatives of the sick and bed-ridden to take a break, by taking advantage of our respite care.'

Lady Amanda nodded happily at being thus informed. 'I have a friend, you see,' she said, 'who is being discharged from hospital on Monday, and I wondered if it was possible for her to spend a week here, to get her strength back up?'

'Absolutely no problem, your ladyship,' the woman informed her, and did another little bob, feeling surprised at herself, for reacting thus. 'I can get someone to show you the rooms we use, so that you can choose which one your friend might prefer, and then, if you could return here, we can sort out the paperwork.'

'Splendid!' declared Lady Amanda, her face breaking out into a beaming smile. Everything was going like clockwork, so far.

A nursing auxiliary was summoned, and led her off down the corridor, opposite to the one where Hugo's and Reggie's room had been situated. At the end of it were two rooms, both with views of the grounds, and in reasonably cheery decorative order.

'I'll just leave you alone here for a while, so that you can make up your mind,' chirped the auxiliary. 'Can you find your own way back to reception?'

'Of course I can, my dear,' cooed Lady Amanda, then muttered, 'Do you think I'm in my dotage yet?' under her breath, as the girl left the room.

It didn't really matter to her, which of the rooms was allotted to Enid, but she supposed the one second from the end would put her slightly nearer any action, and Enid wouldn't mind the faint tang of urine. She looked after her ancient mother who lived with her, and Enid's home always had just a slight whiff of pee. Thus engaged in thought, she heard footsteps coming slowly down the corridor, then another set, moving considerably faster, and a call of, 'Nurse! Nurse Plunkett! Stop this instant!'

The action was about to take place, whatever it was,

right outside the room in which she was standing, so Lady Amanda made herself as still as possible, hardly daring to breathe, in case the two women outside became aware of her presence, and moved their 'business' elsewhere.

'I've just had a complaint from Mr Perkins on Poppy Wing, that, not only did his false teeth taste of soap when you returned them to him, but that they weren't even his own teeth. You'd given him back the wrong set.'

'I can't see how that happened,' replied the meek voice of someone trying to stand their own ground.

'What have you got in that bucket, Nurse Plunkett?' asked the first voice, mean, grating, and easily identifiable as Matron's.

'False teeth,' replied the meek voice, even quieter, knowing that the battle was lost, and Matron was about to scrag her, metaphorically speaking.

'How many times have I told you that you can't just lump all the teeth together in a bucket of soapy water, then run them over with a scrubbing brush?'

'Sorry, Matron. I forgot!'

'Forgot? Stuff and nonsense,' Matron admonished her. 'I know you're only an agency nurse here, but we do have standards and procedures, and they do not include cleaning the patients' false teeth in the manual equivalent of a dishwasher.'

'No, Matron! It won't happen again, Matron.'

'You can bet your shirt on that, Nurse Plunkett, for if I catch you doing this again, I shall send you back to Edwards's Nursing Services with a flea in your ear and a reference that will ring in your mind for ever. Do I make myself clear?'

'Yes, Matron!'

'Then get off to the sluice room, and clean those teeth properly, and get them back to the right patients, if it takes you all day to do it. And start with Mr Perkins. He's got a bag of toffees that he needs them for, although I don't know why; they always gum him up, then he has to ask for help, to get the bottom set unstuck from the top.'

'Yes, Matron!'

Two sets of footsteps disappeared down the corridor in the direction of reception, and Lady Amanda was left alone with her thoughts, again. 'Must remember to tell Enid to clean her own teeth, when she's here. Disgusting! Absolutely disgusting!'

She dawdled back to the reception desk, having noted the number of the room, and proceeded to deal with the form-filling that was necessary to admit Enid Tweedie for a week, then left, to return to Belchester Towers, with a rather amusing tale to relate to Hugo. She must remember to ask him if he had ever had his teeth taken away to be cleaned, while he was staying there.

That evening, at six o'clock sharp, cocktails were served once more, and Hugo decided that this was a part of Manda's life that he could easily get used to. It was not only very civilised, but helped to relax his muscles, where they had been tensed against the pain in his legs. That she had kept up such a daily habit while living on her own amazed him, but he was glad of it.

Sunday was spent teaching Hugo the mysteries of operating the elderly lift that Beauchamp had got back into working order, and although it groaned and creaked alarmingly in its ascents and descents, he had assured them that it was perfectly sound, and safe to use.

Lady Amanda showed Hugo how to open the cage-like doors, and entered with him, to instruct him in the use of the contraption should he wish to visit the first floor. Unfortunately, the lift did not travel up to the second floor, or to the attics, so maybe he'd have to wait until after his raft of mobility-improving operations before being ambitious enough to tackle exploring at those levels.

There was barely room for two people in the little cage,

let alone two stout people, and to begin with they were jammed in back to back, and had to indulge in a perfect fandango of wriggling, to end up both facing front, and in a position to exit the lift, when it reached its destination.

She indicated to Hugo the button that would close the metal doors, then the button which would open them again. Finally, she pointed out the button which would cause the lift to ascend to the first floor. Pressing the 'doors open' button, she instructed Hugo to take them upstairs, as a test of how well he had absorbed her simple instructions.

'I can't, Manda,' he pleaded helplessly. 'The doors are still open.'

'You dolt, Hugo! That's part of using the thing. Close the doors, take us upstairs, then open the doors to let us out. Nothing could be simpler!'

For a few minutes, the lift doors slowly ground closed, then open again: closed, then open again. 'May I suggest that somewhere in the procedure, you actually use the ascend button, Hugo, old bean,' advised Lady Amanda, not cross, but merely amused by his ineptitude.

'I'm terribly sorry, old stick, but I can't seem to remember which button takes us up. Can you just go through the procedure again for me, then I'm sure I shall be able to do it without fault.'

It took a good half hour, but by the end of that time, Hugo was as proficient at ascending and descending in the lift as if he had been operating it all his life. 'I say, old girl, this is jolly rot isn't it, being able to go upstairs without all that darned climbing?' he exclaimed.

'Save your poor old legs no end, won't it?' she offered, in agreement.

Lady Amanda also took him round the various ramps that Beauchamp had restored to their previous positions, and she ascertained that none of them was too steep or too narrow for Hugo to negotiate with his walking frame.

Apart from that, they did little more than take a slow – very slow – toddle in the grounds, and play a few hands of piquet. Monday was to be an unusually busy day, and they both wanted to conserve their strength, for the stamina they would need to find, to get through both Hugo's appointment with the consultant, collecting Enid Tweedie from the hospital ward, and seeing her safely installed in her temporary lodgings.

Lady Amanda had got Beauchamp to drop into the hospital grounds, on their way back from the nursing home, so that she could inform Edith of her upcoming role of 'undercover spy', and why this was necessary; so the stage was set. They had only to wait for curtain-up, the following morning.

Hugo had been offered another lesson in riding the trike, even though he had not yet had the displeasure of actually trying to ride it himself, but had politely refused, and received another stay of execution by the ringing of the telephone.

There was nothing to do now, but wait.

Chapter Six

Monday morning dawned bright and sunny, and they reached the hospital's main entrance with fifteen minutes to spare – just as well, considering how long it would take to get Hugo down the various corridors, and up in the lifts to reach the necessary waiting area. On their way, however, a kindly nurse had seen their difficulty, and promptly fetched them a wheelchair to hasten their progress.

Although Hugo had protested about being pushed around in a bath-chair, like an elderly Edwardian gentleman, the nurse's pretty smile had persuaded him, and she had then volunteered to wheel Hugo to his destination, to Lady Amanda's obvious relief. He was no lightweight, and she was no stripling, and the whole journey through the maze of corridors was leaving her exhausted and disorientated, so that she actually had no idea whether they had been travelling in the correct direction or not.

With the nurse's help, they reached their destination with five minutes to spare, going through the double doors to the waiting area, only for the most ghastly sight to greet their eyes.

Chairs arranged down two sides of the wall contained waiting patients, but all appeared to be liberally doused in blood, and it looked like a massacre had just taken place. Lady Amanda emitted a foghorn-like scream, and Hugo expressed his horror and distress by uttering, 'Oh dear!' and shaking his head from side to side in disbelief.

A distressed nurse, only now noticed by them, was

looking horror-stricken, and paging someone on the in-house telephone, to come to her assistance. In the middle of the floor lay a blood bag – obviously headed somewhere for transfusion – that she must have dropped, loosening its seal. As she explained to them briefly, it had then squirted out its contents in all directions, with the vigour of a deflating balloon, and liberally sprayed all those waiting to see Dr Updyke.

At the sound of the fuss, the great man himself appeared in the doorway of his consulting room, looked around in amazement at the devastation, and the apparently mutilated patients, caught sight of Lady Amanda, and pointed an accusing finger at her.

'You again!' he boomed. 'This is all your doing, isn't it? Call the police, someone! There's a homicidal maniac on the loose. She's had one go at me already, and now she's starting in on my patients.'

Lady Amanda had gazed upon his features with horror, too. That was the bounder who had nearly had her off her trike, if her memory served her correctly. Dr Andrew had told her so, but she'd forgotten all about that. Crumbs! 'Hugo,' she hissed, as quietly as possible. 'That's the cad who wandered in front of my tricycle, and ended up in the shrubbery.'

Hugo had the grace to blush, at this disturbing admission, and hoped this would not be held against him during his consultation. He idly wondered if he ought, or even if he dared, perhaps, to try to get Manda to remain in the waiting area, but he knew this was a non-starter, as soon as the thought entered his head. Manda did as she pleased and, at the moment, she was looking after him, and looking after him meant going in to the doctor's office with him. No go!

It took longer than it should have done to calm down the consultant and explain the situation to him, because he was so wary of Lady Amanda but, finally, all was peaceful again, and it turned out to be Hugo's turn to be seen, which was quite all right with Lady Amanda. That little pantomime had filled in the time they would otherwise have wasted waiting in silence, and been jolly entertaining to boot.

When they were seated in the consulting room, Lady Amanda apologised very prettily for the unfortunate circumstances that had prevailed at their previous meeting, and Dr Updyke thawed a few degrees, from permafrost, to just well-chilled.

She was delighted to note that, when he addressed Hugo, he pronounced his name completely accurately, and she smiled at the consultant, to mark her approval. She had related the trike incident to Hugo on the day he had moved into Belchester Towers, with the post scriptum of her fine for speeding, and he had laughed like a drain, and exclaimed, 'Good old Manda!'

Lady Amanda's smile slightly unnerved Dr Updyke, but he pulled up the e-mail on his computer from Dr Andrew, and began to question him about his current treatment.

'I'm afraid I don't really have any,' apologised Hugo, looking slightly embarrassed at his dearth of pills and potions, as if it were, somehow, his fault. 'My last doctor just told me to take paracetamol, and accept it as part and parcel of old age,' he informed the consultant.

'Outrageous!' Updyke exploded. 'Who exactly was this previous doctor of yours?'

'Dr Anstruther,' Hugo stated, and both he and Lady Amanda watched as the medical man turned scarlet with wrath.

'Silly old fool should either have retired, or been struck off the Medical Register years ago. The real toll of the harm he's done will never be uncovered, but his treatment of you is typical of the man. He's too old to care, too old to understand modern treatments, and only carries on for the money. Disgraceful!'

The doctor had now thawed completely, and examined Hugo with the tenderness of a mother examining her child. 'Right, Mr Cholmondley-Crichton-Crump, I'm going to send you off for some X-rays now, and for blood tests. I want to see you again in a week. The receptionist in the waiting area will make a follow-up appointment for you.

'In the meantime, I'm going to give you a prescription which you can have filled at the hospital pharmacy, for some jolly strong painkillers and some anti-inflammatory pills. They should ease things for you, and we can follow on from there. I have a fair idea of what the X-rays will show, and I have to warn you that it could be a double hip-replacement and a double knee-replacement for you.

'If this proves so, it will take some time – maybe a year or two – to get everything done, but I can assure you that it will give you a completely new lease of life. If you have any questions, make a note of them, and bring them along to your next appointment, which I sincerely hope,' here, Dr Updyke paused to give a little chuckle, 'will not commence with a bloodbath. Haha!'

He shook hands as they left, in quite a good humour, and it was only as they made to exit his consulting room, that his expression turned to a slight frown of puzzlement. That woman had seemed perfectly OK today, but what was she? Some kind of Jekyll and Hyde personality? When she had come roaring at him on that tricycle of hers, she had looked just like a Valkyrie in full flight. Today she had been as polite as was to be expected, given who she was, and her station in life. He just hoped that he never had the misfortune to encounter the Valkyrie side of her personality again.

The wheelchair had been left in the waiting area, and was still there when they came out. The receptionist, having noticed how slowly Hugo walked into the consulting room, had kindly summoned a porter to push him to wherever he was fated to go next.

Clutching his fistful of forms and the prescription, Hugo lowered himself gratefully into the seat, and made his trips to the X-ray department, to have his blood taken, and to the hospital pharmacy, with un-hoped for swiftness, and they found themselves back at Belchester Towers in time for lunch, a goal believed unattainable by Lady Amanda, when they had set out on their trip, earlier.

A short nap after lunch to eliminate the rigours of the morning, saw them awake and alert again, at three o'clock, and preparing to go to collect Enid from her hospital discharge, and settle her in at the home.

When they located Enid's bed in Robin Ward, she was already dressed, and sitting on a bedside chair, her bag packed and waiting beside her, her discharge papers clutched in her right hand.

'The doctor came round early,' she excused herself for being ready to leave before time. 'I've been sitting here for almost an hour.'

'Do you good to be out of bed,' commented Lady Amanda, gruffly and unsympathetically. 'By the way, I don't think you've met my long-lost friend Hugo,' she stated, having noticed Enid staring at Hugo in an interrogatory way. She rarely saw Lady Amanda in company with a gentleman friend, and she was naturally curious.

'May I introduce you to Hugo Cholmondley-Crichton-Crump?' Enid was fascinated to meet someone with such an exotic-sounding name, and even more so, when Lady Amanda wrote it down for her to see.

'So it's pronounced as you said it, but it's spelled like this?' she asked incredulously.

'That's right, Enid.'

'I've never met anyone before who had a name that sounded differently to what it looked like on paper,' she added, in wonder.

'Well, you have now, so come on, let's get weaving. Now, you know that you're our eyes and ears in that home, don't you? Good! We need to find out who was impersonating Reggie's nephew, what he looked like, and – if you're really good at this – where he might have come across Reggie, to pull a fast one on him and the staff there, like that. Got it? Good!'

The hospital provided a nurse to wheel Enid to the main hospital doors in a chair, and she then transferred into the Rolls, evidently enjoying herself immensely, and acting like Lady Bountiful, as she climbed into the vintage vehicle.

Their destination was only a couple of hundred yards away, but that didn't stop Enid savouring every second of it. Being in a Rolls-Royce wasn't an everyday occurrence for her, and she noticed how people stopped and stared at it, as it passed. Lucky, lucky, Lady Amanda! And she just took this sort of thing for granted!

At The Birdlings, she was clearly delighted with her room, and the thought that she could just take it easy for a week, and be waited on, hand foot and finger – something she had not appreciated in the hospital, due to the way she had felt after her operation, and the fact that the hospital kitchens seemed to have a contract with the operating theatre staff, regarding the provision of meat. There had been far too much offal on the menu for her liking, anything including meat had been unidentifiable, and had left her feeling very suspicious of the source of their butchery requisitions.

After having been shown the room, and its meagre facilities, Lady Amanda turned on Enid and said, 'I suggest that you try speaking to Nurse Plunkett. She doesn't seem very happy here, and has been sent by an agency. I think she'd be willing to give you any of the dirt she knows about on this place, just for the sheer pleasure of it.'

'I'll do my best,' responded Enid Tweedie, looking slightly worried, now she was actually installed here and on the job, so to speak.

'You will do better than that, Enid. You will make me proud of you!' was Lady Amanda's uncompromising reply, and was not so much a prediction, as an order. 'We'll visit every day – don't want to trust important information in a case of murder to the phone lines. Don't know who might be listening in,' she added, somewhat melodramatically, in Hugo's opinion. This wasn't Sexton Blake: this was real life, and real life was safer than fiction, or so he thought, then.

When they finally returned to Belchester Towers, it was too late for afternoon tea, so Lady Amanda requested that dinner be brought forward a little, to compensate, and Hugo announced that he needed another little lie-down, as it was some time since he had been so active.

'Really, Hugo! You spent most of the time we were at the hospital being pushed around in that wheelchair. How can you possibly be tired again?' Lady Amanda asked, casting a sceptical eye over him, and realising that he really did look worn out. 'Never mind! Can't be helped! Off you toddle, and don't worry about me. I'll find something to occupy my time,' at which point the old pull-style front door bell rang, and she exclaimed in triumph, 'Here we go. I said something would turn up.'

The something that turned up was a representative from the Social Services department, with a wheelchair for Hugo to use, until such time as he was more mobile. 'Dr Andrew phoned and ordered it,' the gentleman at the door explained. 'If you'd just like to sign here – and here – and here? Thank you very much, madam.'

'That's 'my lady' to you,' she informed him haughtily, and took charge of Hugo's new chariot. 'Hey, Chummy, just before you toddle off to bed, look what Dr Andrew's sent round for you. Fantastic, eh?'

'If you like that sort of thing,' replied Hugo, turning his back and shuffling off in the direction of his bedroom, which was where he liked it – on the ground floor, where he felt safest.

Abandoning the new carriage, which Beauchamp could take care of, as far as finding somewhere to stash it was concerned, Lady Amanda arranged her face in a determined expression, removed an old crash helmet of Mummy's from a cupboard, and stumped purposefully off, out of the house, and towards the stables.

She was determined to get the hand of the motorised trike while Hugo was napping. She'd had Beauchamp try it out himself, leaving any alterations or improvements to its running in his capable hands, and was now ready to get 'back on the horse' so to speak. It may have beaten her once, but it wouldn't be given another chance. She would master it, or die in the attempt.

When Hugo entered the drawing room after his nap, still a little bleary-eyed, he found Lady Amanda sitting on a sofa, her hair wildly out of place, oil smudges on her face and hands, and a triumphant expression on her face.

'Been taming the wild beast,' she said, by way of explanation, and when Hugo's face broke into a study of incomprehension, explained in more detail:

'That motorised tricycle that Beauchamp fixed up for you. I've had him do a few alterations, and I've just about mastered driving the thing. It's nowhere near as excitable as it was last time we had it out, and I think it's time you learned to ride it.

'Oh, not now, you silly,' she added, watching fear creep across his features. 'Maybe tomorrow, before we go to visit Enid for her fist debrief of the case. We won't go until after lunch – give her time to settle in, so there'll be plenty of time in the morning. The funeral's not till

Wednesday, so we've got time on our hands, and nothing planned to fill it. Are you up for it, old chap?'

'Only if you ride it first, so that I can see it's not wild and dangerous, as it was when you tried it out before.'

'Of course I'll demonstrate,' she assured him, pleased to be able to demonstrate how proficient she had become at controlling the bloody-minded contraption in so short a time. 'I'll give you a performance, explain everything, then you can have a go – and if you wear Daddy's old crash helmet, we should be prepared, in the event of a mishap.'

Hugo didn't like the sound of this last bit, but he was game to try it out, and nodded in agreement before his hostess went on, not waiting for a spoken answer from him.

'Six o'clock, and time for a bit of a belter, I think, don't you, Hugo?' This was another rhetorical question, and Hugo wisely recognised it and remained silent. He'd have to get used to those rhetorical doo-dahs again. 'Where's that Beau ... Oh, there you are! I didn't hear you come in. *Quelle surprise*! Now, pass the tray to Hugo first as he's a guest, then I'll have mine. Thank you very much, Beauchamp.'

As the manservant left the room, he was heard to mutter, 'And my name's pronounced Beecham!'

Chapter Seven

Hugo was delighted, on waking on Tuesday morning, to find that the weather had taken a turn for the worse, and rain was falling relentlessly from a leaden sky. 'Hoorah!' he thought. Now he wouldn't have to have a go on that three-wheeled machine from hell. Manda would have to let him off, because of the weather. There was nothing even *she* could do about that.

Lady Amanda did try to persuade Hugo that they could manage perfectly well if she attached an umbrella to the back of the thing, but Hugo was having none of it. 'The wind's getting up,' he pointed out to her, 'and if the brolly gets caught by a gust, I'm going to look like ET, flying on that thing, or Mary Poppins in the Tour de France, heaven forbid.'

'You win, Chummy. We'll have to postpone it till after the funeral now,' she conceded with bad grace, 'But there's nothing stopping us having a few games of cards, and then we can have a quiet read until lunchtime.'

This suited Hugo's ambitions perfectly, and they played a few rounds of gin rummy, before putting away the playing cards. Hugo then settled down with his newspaper, while Lady Amanda sat at a small table, her hands occasionally darting forward to write something on a piece of paper resting on the table in front of her.

Hugo was quite happily absorbed in his reading, but was disturbed, every minute or so, by a cry of 'Aha', or 'Of course, how stupid of me'.

'What on earth are you up to, old girl?' he asked a trifle querulously.

'Crossword, old stick,' she replied, without looking up.

'But you haven't got a paper?' he observed, logically.

'People put them through the door for me. Cut from their newspapers. They know how addicted I am, and this way I get crosswords from a good cross-section of the papers. Good, eh? Did you know that the French word for a paperclip is "trombone"? Super clue!'

'Perhaps you could moderate your ejaculations, Manda, old girl,' he suggested. 'Keep losing my thread, with you yelling all over the place.'

'Sorry, I'll try to keep it down, but it's just so exciting when I solve a particularly tricky cryptic clue. I'll try just to wave my fist in the air, in future, so as not to disturb your reading.'

Which she did, but Hugo could see it out of the corner of his eye, and found it just as distracting as her yells of triumph had been. Finally, he gave up, placed the open newspaper over his face, and dozed off to sleep. If he was sleeping, at least her raised fists of triumph couldn't disturb his dreams.

After a very satisfying half-hour's nap, Hugo woke up refreshed, and asked, apropos of nothing in particular, 'So you never married either, old girl?'

Lady Amanda looked up from her crossword, and prepared her answer. 'No, Hugo. Of course, I danced with all and sundry during my coming-out year, but, after one disastrous incident, I only ever took one walk in the garden, during a ball.'

'What happened to put you off, old thing?' Hugo was interested now.

'Some boy or other – I can't remember who he was, now – took me outside for a walk by moonlight, and the bounder grabbed me round the waist and kissed me full on the mouth, and actually stuck his tongue down my throat. I was so disgusted I threw up in a rose bush, so I never went for a "walk" again. Gardens contain too many dangerous things, like shrubberies and summer-houses. I really can't be doing with anything wet and sticky, unless it's called "pudding".

'What about you, Hugo? I never fell for that old rot about not taking the chance on having your name lengthened again. That sort of tosh simply won't wash with me. That was a load of old cow poo; a load of doggy-doodles. Out with it! What was the real reason?'

'Same sort of thing, really. I was taken outside by a girl, and she kissed me, and put my hand ... somewhere about her person, and I nearly passed out. I'm with you on that one.

'We danced together at a ball once, didn't we?'

'I do believe we did. And at one time, I had a tiny crush on you, Hugo – when you used to visit, in the school holidays. '

'Never!'

'I did. And then I took that ill-fated "walk" in the garden, and I decided I was finished with the opposite sex. Everything's so untidy and undignified in human relationships, and I didn't want to have any part in that sort of thing.'

'Good for you, Manda. I felt absolutely the same about it. Changing the subject somewhat – we've got so much to catch up on, haven't we? Did you have a good time at school? I didn't. I was always being bullied for being, what they call nowadays, a bit of a wimp.'

'Oh, I had a shocking time. I was sent somewhere up north, to be educated along with the lumpen daughters of the aristocratic sod – and right sods they were too – please excuse my language.'

'Don't mention it,' remarked Hugo politely.

'Horrible little beasts they were. Always going on about their ponies, and the gymkhanas they'd ridden in. And when they found out where I came from, they gave me no peace. Separated Belchester into "Belch" and "ester", and from then on, I was known as Windy Esther. Sadistic little sods they were. Children can be so cruel! It was such a relief to come home for the holidays, to some civilised company.'

'I notice you don't use much of the house, nowadays, do you, Manda?'

'Most of it's locked up; the furniture all dust-sheeted. Why?'

'Well, I wonder you don't open it to the public. It'd give you a real purpose in life, and it would bring in a few extra shekels.'

'I've thought about it from time to time, but it all seems a bit too much like hard work.'

'Well, there are two of us, now. Maybe it's something we can organise together.'

'Not until you've had all your treatment and are a bit more mobile, Hugo. If we tried it now, I'd be the one doing all the running around, and you'd be almost chair-bound.'

'True, but it's something to consider for the future, what?'

'Maybe!'

After luncheon, they donned their wet weather gear, to venture out to visit Enid Tweedie, to see if she'd managed to gather any useful information with reference to identifying old Reggie's mystery visitor. Rain still fell from the sky in torrents, and Lady Amanda rather hoped that it would clear up before the morrow, for there was nothing more likely to induce a deep depression, than standing by a muddy graveside in the rain, forced to contemplate one's own mortality.

The home smelt of boiled Brussels sprouts today, or at least, that's what Lady Amanda hoped it was! They found Enid sitting in an armchair by the window of her room, engrossed in a ladies magazine of the trashier type, and she put it down reluctantly, at their arrival.

First things first: 'How are you, Enid? Good, good! And who's looking after your mother while you're in here? Come to mention it, who looks after her during your frequent stays in hospital?'

'She goes to my sister down near the college,' Enid replied, and then to avoid further questioning about her domestic arrangements, added, 'And Mrs Next-Door feeds the cat.'

'So your house is empty, then?'

'That's right.'

'Better give me the keys, so I can check you haven't been burgled. We wouldn't want you coming out of here and finding your house ransacked, now would we?'

'Good idea, Lady Amanda. They're in my handbag. I'll just get them for you.'

While she scrabbled around in her handbag looking for her keys, Lady Amanda whispered to Hugo, 'If I can get into her house, at least I can give it a good airing – throw all the windows and doors open, when the weather's a bit better. What with her old mother and the cat, the house simply reeks of 'wee wee' and old pussy.'

Transferring the unexpectedly large bunch of keys into her own handbag, Lady Amanda enquired, 'Have you had a chance to talk to that Nurse Plunkett yet?'

'What a very nice young lady she is!' stated Enid, with a happy smile. 'Always has time to stop and chat; not like some of the others, who are always rushing off to do something or other.'

'What have you learned?'

'That she works for Edwards's Nursing Services, and she's pretty fed-up with being placed here on her own. Quite often the nurses are on temporary contract in couples or threesomes, when it's for a hospital, but Matron here wouldn't hear of having to pay for a second nurse, so she only took the one.'

'That's all very nice to know, but we're trying to place that chap who posed as Reggie's nephew, not extract her woes and troubles from her.'

'I do realise that, and I was just setting the scene, before I got to the interesting bit,' Enid replied, a trifle sniffily. 'She did say that she'd spotted one of the other agency workers here, when she came to look round the place and be interviewed, but he hadn't seen her. She assumed he was visiting someone, as he was carrying a bunch of flowers.'

'Aha!' exclaimed Lady Amanda. 'Does she know his name?'

'She can't remember, for the moment, but said if I was really interested, she'd phone one of her colleagues, and find out for me. It seems he was employed six months or so ago, to nurse an elderly gentleman in his home, but that contract ended, and he's had to move on since then.'

'Aha!' Lady Amanda exclaimed again. 'That's the bunny! I'm sure about it now.'

'How can you be?' asked Hugo, doubtfully. 'You've only got one tiny bit of information.'

'By using the old noggin, Hugo. This chap nurses Reggie, gets him to change his will, then Reggie has to move here. Our chappie then starts to call in on him, to make sure he hasn't been lucid enough to change his will again, and then, for some currently unknown reason, bumps him off. There!'

'There's a lot of conjecture in there, Manda. Mind out! You might get your fingers burnt, if you try accusing an innocent man of murder.'

'Piffle!' she replied. 'I know I'm right! I can feel it in my water.'

'There's a visitor's loo just across the corridor,' they were informed by Enid, 'should you feel the need.'

After their now habitual cocktails, and dinner, Lady

72

Amanda started to look shifty, and began fidgeting in an altogether embarrassed way that Hugo did not at all understand. 'Whatever's got into you, old thing?' he asked, concerned. 'You look as if all the hounds of hell are after you.'

'I have to do something tonight – with Beauchamp,' she explained, looking terribly uncomfortable.

There was a pause, and then Hugo exclaimed, 'Oh, not that, surely? And with Beauchamp? But you said earlier …' His voice trailed off.

Pulling herself into a very upright position, and assuming a haughty expression, Lady Amanda replied, 'Hugo, wash your mouth out with soap and water. I can read your mind, and it's positively pornographic. It's nothing like that, I can assure you.'

With a jaundiced eye, Hugo retorted, 'Well, what is it then, if it's "nothing like that"?'

Walking towards him and leaning over – a movement which both startled and alarmed him, she pointed at her head and said, 'Being a man, you probably haven't noticed anything amiss, but my hair is turning from blonde to grey, from the roots out.' Here, she lowered her voice to a whisper, 'I have my roots dyed once a month. Can't afford the hairdresser, so Beauchamp does it for me. Much cheaper that way, and it stops all the nosy parkers talking about how my hair isn't its natural colour. *Comprende, senor?*'

'Oh, got you, old girl!' exclaimed Hugo in complete understanding. 'So there is a chink in your armour after all, then?'

'Not so much a chink, as the merest speck of vanity. Now, I'm off upstairs to the bathroom with Beauchamp, and I'll probably not come down again, so sleep well, old stick.'

'Same to you, Manda.'

'And remember – not a word to a soul about this, Hugo.

73

I'm relying on your discretion.'

'I'm loyal to the end, old friend,' he said, saluting her as she left the room.

Lady Amanda left the room and stumped off upstairs to meet her fate. Stopping in her bedroom, she stripped to the waist, and hurriedly wrapped her upper half in large, camouflaging towels, held together with old-fashioned wooden clothes pegs, before presenting herself in the bathroom.

The bathroom itself was so old-fashioned that it had become, now, high fashion again, with its cast iron roll-top bath with lion's feet and 'telephone' hand-shower attachment. The ceramic sink was oblong, with cut corners, and still had the original taps, and the lavatory was the high cistern flush-type, decorated with blue leaves and flowers, and a bumble bee in the pan for the gentlemen to aim at.

In fact, a photograph of it would not have looked out of place in any home-design magazine. Lady Amanda, of course, realised this, and had stopped moaning about renewing the old suite a couple of years ago, when she realised just how trendy her bathroom was.

Beauchamp had everything laid out, and she took her seat in the chair he had provided, with her usual trepidation. Although Beauchamp had been providing this service for several years now, she still felt (and indeed was) naked under the towels, in the presence of a man, and she was very unnerved, every time her roots had to be coloured.

Beauchamp was the soul of discretion, of course – she had no worries on that front. It was just the sensation of nakedness, which she knew was stupid. She was naked under her clothes in his presence every day, and just considered herself decently attired – but this – this just felt different, and made her very uneasy, as if the towels were transparent, or even invisible, leaving her top half exposed for him to ogle.

'Silly old trout!' she muttered to herself, and gave Beauchamp permission to go ahead and apply the stinking stuff to her roots with the harsh-bristled root-brush. Later, when it was dry and combed again, all these negative feelings would be as if they had never existed, but, for an hour or so, every month, she felt like a threatened virgin, and there was no 'again' about it.

While she was 'cooking', Beauchamp kindly fetched her reading glasses and her bedtime book from her room, and left her alone for half an hour, until she was nicely done to a turn, when he would return, and rinse and condition her curly locks, all blonde again, and without a tell-tale trace of grey.

While she was thus on her own, Lady Amanda had what until recently she had taken so much for granted – some time on her own. Although it was lovely to have Hugo staying with her at The Towers, she had lived alone since Mummy and Daddy died – Beauchamp didn't count. He had always been there. But now she was beginning to realise how difficult it was to adapt to having someone else about the place.

Of course, it wasn't Hugo's fault, and she couldn't let him go back to that ghastly home, but it was going to take some time to establish a routine that satisfied them both, with time together, and time in solitude. She knew Hugo had also lived alone before, and he must be feeling very much as she was, but she was sure they could work something out between them.

Chapter Eight

At breakfast the next morning, served half an hour earlier than usual, so that they should have sufficient time to make themselves ready for Reggie's funeral, they discussed what they wanted to achieve that morning.

'Being at the funeral will give us a good chance to have a real eyeful of whoever attends, then, I understand, it's back to Reggie's house for the wake. Young Mr Williams has sort of given me permission to stay on for the reading of the will, and I want to know to whom the dosh has been left.'

'Where did Reggie live?' asked Hugo.

'Apparently he lived in that really old house called High Hedges – the only property that fronts on to The Butts. I've passed it many a time on my peregrinations on the trike, but never realised it was Reggie's place. If I had, I'd have called in to say hello, and now it's too late.' Lady Amanda drew a handkerchief from her pocket and mopped at the corners of her eyes.

'There, there, Manda. Never mind. You might not have got to meet up with him again, for all your efforts visiting the nursing home, but at least you sussed out that he'd been murdered, and are going to avenge his death now, by hunting down and bringing to justice the cad who knocked him off,' replied Hugo in soothing tones, but somewhat pompously.

'*We* are going to bring that bounder to justice, Hugo – *us* – both of us.'

'Fair enough, but I don't see what a useless old buffer like me can do to help apprehend a dangerous criminal.'

'Just do as I tell you and you won't go far wrong,' Lady Amanda instructed him.

'Don't I always!' replied Hugo, helping himself to another slice of toast and the thick-cut marmalade.

'If I take my mobile phone with me,' she informed her companion, 'I might be able to get a photo of that *faux* nephew, and then we can show it to Nurse Plunkett, for identification purposes, and then … Well, we can get the case wrapped up fairly rapidly, and present it all to that ill-mannered Inspector Moody – I rang up to check who was on duty when I called in – and show him who are the better detectives.'

'It's all a bit Enid Blyton, isn't it, Manda?' Hugo ventured.

'Tosh! Easy as one, two, three. We'll show that uncivilised buffoon at the police station who knows their onions and who doesn't.'

'Well, just be careful. If that chap's killed once, he may not hesitate to do it again,' Hugo warned, suddenly fearful for her safety – suddenly fearful for his own safety, too, when push came to shove. He'd momentarily forgotten that they were working together.

In the car, on the way to St Michael-in-the-Fields, Lady Amanda informed Hugo that his house was on the rental market. 'But you don't even know where I live!' he exclaimed in amazement. 'I never said anything, when you were referring to the old place, and how lovely it had been. Didn't like to. Shatter your illusions, and all that.'

'Well, I have a little confession to make,' she told him.

'What have you done now?' he asked, in a resigned tone of voice.

'Oh, nothing much. I'd already worked out that you'd moved on. I lifted your house keys from your jacket pocket one day when you were having a little nap. It's very naughty of you to have an address label on them. It's just asking to be robbed.'

'I hadn't thought of that,' replied Hugo. 'It was so that they could be returned to me, if I ever lost them.'

'You were more likely to be cleaned out, or murdered in your bed – or both!' chided Lady Amanda, amazed at the naïveté of her old friend.

'Holy Moses! So you could've saved my life!'

'Better than that,' she said. 'I phoned round a selection of local estate agents, and got Beauchamp to sort out access – I'm afraid he had to have a few copies of the keys made, but we'll get them all back before anyone moves in. Anyway, they've all valued it for rental, and I've chosen the one who has come up with the most believable figure, and the lowest rate of commission, and I've asked him to advertise it.'

'But ...'

'But me no buts, Hugo. You don't have to do anything. If there's anything you'd like to remove from the property, Beauchamp and I can sort that out. The same with any special pieces of furniture that you'd like put into storage – loads of room at Belchester Towers – and the agent does all the financial checks, collects the rent, and just pays it into your account. All you have to do is sit back and accrue the profits.'

'But what if something needs doing?'

'The agent organises all that, and takes it out of the rent money,' she explained, feeling that she had adequately clarified the process to him by now.

'I say! You have been a busy little bee, haven't you, Manda?'

'I do my level best. I used to hang around the estate manager's office, when we had more land, and tenants, so I had a fair idea of how things worked.'

There were only a handful of people in the church for the funeral. Young Mr Williams was there as Reggie's legal representative here on this earth, there were a couple of people from the nursing home that Lady Amanda recognised, and a couple who introduced themselves as Reggie's former neighbours. The only other person in attendance was a man who appeared to be in his mid-thirties, who sat in the front row, his face shaded by the hat he had not had the respect and courtesy to remove, inside the church.

It was black! The hat was black! 'There you go, Hugo,' whispered Lady Amanda. 'It's always the man in the black hat who's the baddie.'

'Don't be silly, Manda. That's only in old films and westerns. He's at a funeral. Of course his hat is black.'

'I bet that's the fake nephew!' she hissed back, right into his ear, which tickled a lot, and he had to push her away, while he gave it a good old rub with the palm of his hand, to stop it itching so.

'Shut up and behave yourself!' was his last word on the matter, and they both bent their heads to examine the flimsy piece of paper which contained the order of service. Hugo had barely had sufficient time to take in the details, when she hissed at him again. 'That Moody man should be here, not us!'

'Who the hell is "that moody man"?' asked Hugo, a little tetchily.

'That policeman – Inspector Moody. If only he'd listened to me instead of humiliating me, he could be sitting in the church now, about to pounce on the villain.'

In uncharacteristically demotic mode, Hugo hissed back, 'Can it, sweetheart! It's all about to go off!'

The service itself was short and swift, and started with a couple of verses of 'For Those in Peril on the Sea'. 'Reggie wasn't a sailor, was he?' whispered Hugo, behind his hand.

'Not to my knowledge. I know he was passed unfit for service during the war, and I never heard of him having a boat of any kind.'

The eulogy was short and evidently delivered by a clergyman who had never met the dear departed. Both Lady Amanda and Hugo were surprised that the man they had dubbed the *faux* nephew hadn't risen to speak, but, on more considered thought, realised he probably knew very little about Reggie, being a fake.

Two verses of 'The Day Thou Gavest Lord is Over' finished the swiftest funeral that either one of them had ever been to, and the undertaker's men came in, to ferry the coffin to the graveside.

They made a very sad and sorry bunch – the few of them that there were – standing in the pouring rain and getting soaked to the skin – as the coffin was lowered into the ground, and the clergyman began to say the words of the service of committal. When the time came for someone to throw in a handful of earth, they all looked round at each other, Lady Amanda finally removing her gloves and picking up a handful of almost liquid mud, before pouring it into the grave, to dribble across the coffin, like the trail of a brown snail.

The man in the black hat blushed with embarrassment, and reluctantly copied her action, as did Hugo, as a mark of respect for the departed. The vicar made the sign of the cross, and they all looked around to see who would be the first to leave.

As it happened, it was the man who had sat at the front and claimed to be related to Reggie who scuttled off first, but that was no problem, as there was to be a wake – a very small one, by the looks of it – afterwards, and all Lady Amanda and Hugo had to do was to get Beauchamp to follow the car of Reggie's ex-neighbours, to their unknown destination.

'Actually, I think it would be better to follow young Mr Williams. The neighbours might not be going back to wherever it is – it could be the young man's house. I hope it is, because then we will at least know where he lives. But, if we follow young Mr Williams, we know he'll be going back afterwards, because he's arranged to read the will, after the – the – whatever it turns out to be.

'I don't expect a champagne reception, but a cup of tea and a slice of cake, or a ham sandwich would go down well. It's getting on for lunchtime, or will be by the time we've all gathered there, and I shall, no doubt, be ravenous.'

'Typical Manda!' commented Hugo. 'You always did put your stomach first!'

'Anyway, I've got a thirst on, after all that singing!'

'Pathetic, wasn't it?' Hugo asked, looking round at her for a response.

'It certainly was: a sad and pathetic end to a man's life, and if there's nothing more we can do about it, we'll at least expose the person who caused him to be planted in the ground today.'

'Oh, damn and blast it!' exclaimed Lady Amanda, as the car in front of them turned into the drive of Reggie's old house in The Butts. 'How are we ever going to find out where this cove lives, if he holds the wake at Reggie's old house?'

'Haven't the faintest idea, old thing, but I'm sure you'll think of something,' replied Hugo with confidence.

'Oh, I will, I will. And if I can't get the information today, there are more ways than one to skin a cat.'

'You think this chap's got a cat, do you?' asked Hugo, not really paying attention any more.

'You're dothering, Hugo. It's just a figure of speech, as you jolly well know.'

Young Mr Williams did the honours at the front door, welcoming them all back to Reggie's old home, which seemed very odd, considering there was a 'relative' in attendance. Where had that fellow got to, wondered Lady

Amanda? He ought, at least, to act the part, by welcoming the funeral guests. But he was nowhere to be seen, nor did he appear as they sipped glasses of warm, cheap punch, and nibbled on curling ham and cheese sandwiches.

It wasn't until Reggie's next-door neighbours left, that he reappeared, but he moved to the far side of the room, and seemed to take an inordinate interest in a bookcase full of dusty leather-bound volumes, that probably had not been taken out of the shelves in years – nay, decades.

'What's he up to?' asked Hugo, *sotto voce.*

'Avoiding speaking to anyone, if you ask me. He's pulling that old trick of trying to hide in plain view, like that purloined letter, or whatever it was, that Sherlock Holmes had to sort out.'

'He can't hide for ever.'

'Probably waiting for us to go. What he doesn't know is that I arranged with young Mr Williams for us to stay on and hear the will being read. That should spike his guns good and proper! Watch this!'

And with this last imperative hissed at Hugo, she approached the rear view of the man who wasn't who he said he was. 'You're dear old Reggie's nephew, aren't you?' she asked, in the sort of piercing voice that simply cannot be ignored, and he had to turn towards his interrogator, no doubt flabbergasted at being addressed as such.

His first reaction was one of alarm, and he simply blurted out, 'Who told you that?' Lady Amanda was on dangerous ground here, but it had not occurred to her that her manner of address might make him suspicious of her motives for being here.

'Can't remember. I just remember hearing that you were,' she assured him. 'Had a great old time in the navy, didn't he, your uncle, during the war?'

'Really enjoyed himself,' came the answer, with great assurance, an utter and complete lie. He was handling himself well under fire.

'Well, nice to meet you,' she said, 'Although, I suppose our paths will never cross again after today,' she finished, turning away, and thinking, until we bring you to justice, that is.

Her hearing was still sharp, though, and, as she left his side, she heard him mutter, 'I damned well hope they don't!'

Young Mr Williams had overheard this exchange, and frowned in puzzlement. He'd have to try to remember to have a word with young Lady Amanda sometime. The poor girl seemed to have got her wires crossed somehow.

As the few remaining guests trickled away, young Mr Williams began to shuffle through the papers in his briefcase, and when there were only 'the suspect', Lady Amanda and Hugo left, he cleared his throat and begged for them to be seated. 'I have here the last will and testament made by Mr Reginald Chamberlain Pagnell, and I propose to read it to you now.'

'Why are those two still here?' asked the suspected murderer.

'Because we're old family friends!' boomed Lady Amanda, in her best Lady Bracknell voice. That quelled him, and the reading of the will proceeded.

After a number of small bequests, it was announced that the residual legatee was a Mr Richard Churchill Myers, of number six Wilmington Crescent, Belchester, another old friend, apparently.

Lady Amanda fixed her beadily accusing eye at the young man sitting with them, and enquired if this were he, to which he replied, smugly, in the negative, and stood, preparatory to leaving.

'Is that *really* not you?' she enquired again of the young man.

''Fraid not!' he admitted, and gave her a cheesy grin of triumph. How had he managed to outwit them? Lady

Amanda was simply furious.

'Dammit!' she muttered, rather strongly for her, and nudged Hugo to get him moving. 'I've left Beauchamp outside with the Rolls. Told him to use my mobile to try to get a picture of the cove leaving. We'll just have to follow him now, if we want to find out where he lives.'

'But there was nothing left to him in the will. We've hit a dead end,' protested Hugo. 'If he wasn't left a bean, why would he want to kill old Reggie like that? It doesn't make sense, Manda.'

'It does!' she insisted. 'It's just a complicated puzzle, for which we don't have all the pieces yet. I *know* that young man did for Reggie, and I have the evidence locked securely in my safe to prove it. We'll just have to find out who he really is.'

'Perhaps he was Reggie's home nurse,' suggested Hugo, rather swamped with things medical at the moment and not enjoying it one jot.

''Brilliant!' quoth Lady Amanda, and rushed to catch young Mr Williams before he left. She managed to grab him by the sleeve of his jacket as he was heading out of the room, and asked, in as casual a fashion at she could muster at short notice, and with such excitement flooding her mind, 'Who is that young man who stayed on for the reading of the will? I don't think I've been introduced.'

'That was young Mr Foster – Derek Foster,' he answered, unsuspectingly.

'And how did he know Reggie?' she asked, her face a mask of innocence.

'I believe he used to provide nursing care for Mr Pagnell, before the departed had to be admitted to a home for full-time care. His mind was wandering so much he needed constant supervision, lest he wander away and get lost, I believe.'

'That's very interesting, Mr Williams. Thank you so much for your time and trouble. Do you happen to know where Mr Foster lives?' This would really be a coup for them, if she could get his address.

'I'm afraid I haven't the faintest idea, my dear young lady. He answered an advertisement I placed in the local paper, asking him to contact us. This, he did, and our only other contact has been by telephone.'

'Cow poo!' declared Lady Amanda, as they got back into the Rolls. 'I thought we had it all neatly stitched up there, and now we've lost him. Waiting to talk to that old twit has cost us time we couldn't afford. If I'd thought about it harder, it would probably have been better to follow him to find out his address, then we could have delivered him to Inspector Moody as a nicely wrapped-up parcel, specifically addressed to the Department of Public Prosecutions.'

'But he didn't get the money or the house,' protested Hugo anew.

'No, but he was Reggie's home nurse. There's more of a tangled plot here, than I thought. Did you manage to get a photograph, Beauchamp?'

'I shot off a couple, and one of them's not too bad. He moved in the other one, and he's just a blur.'

'Good-oh!' chortled Lady Amanda. 'A very successful surveillance job, Beauchamp!'

'Beecham,' muttered their chauffeur, but under his breath.

'So, what do we do next, Manda?' asked Hugo, all ears, now that the game was still afoot.

'We show the photograph on my phone to Nurse Plunkett, to see if she can positively identify him, and we proceed from there. It's time we visited Enid again, anyway. I promised we'd visit her every day, and I've not been too good at keeping my promise.'

Chapter Nine

The weather cleared up after luncheon, and a watery sun shone in a pale blue sky. This was grist to Lady Amanda's mill, and she insisted that Hugo have another go at learning to ride the motorised trike. His protest were squashed as easily as swatting a fly, and at two thirty he found himself being escorted outside, wearing an old-fashioned crash helmet, and a pair of gauntlets – 'Lest you fall off and scrape your hands,' Lady Amanda had reassured him.

Except that all this protective gear just made him even more apprehensive about the venture, but he knew there was no escape. Once Manda had you in her clutches, there was no way out. A man resigned to his fate, he allowed himself to be led over to 'that contraption of Satan himself', as he mentally referred to it; but never out loud, for fear that Manda should hear him, and brand him a coward.

'Get on it, then you can just try pedalling, without turning the motor on, just to get the feel of the steering; that sort of thing,' she commanded him. And he did push like the very devil on the pedals, but they moved so very slowly, that Lady Amanda eventually took hold of the back of the saddle, and started to push him, to get him going.

'Don't do that, Manda! It's too fast!'

'Stuff and nonsense! Here, let me push you a little faster – feet on pedals, old boy,' she puffed, heaving him along with all her strength, her hands now firmly on his back.

'Argh!' screamed Hugo, as his feet met the pedals, and found the turning movement irresistible, and were compelled to join in. 'Manda!' he wailed, 'You forgot to tell me where the brakes are.' And thus, hooting and yelling, he propelled himself, slowly but assuredly, into the trunk of a venerable oak tree.

Luckily, he had been travelling at a very low speed, and neither he nor the tricycle came to any harm. 'Now, Hugo,' ordered Lady Amanda bossily, 'here are the brakes, just under your hands on the handlebar.' She pointed at each brake handle. 'Have you never ridden a bicycle before? It's just the same as that.'

'A skill, I'm ashamed to say, I never mastered,' admitted the hapless jockey.

'You just squeeze them gently, and you'll come to a stop. When the motor's going, you just turn this little knob, then activate the brakes.'

'I don't think I want to try it with the motor today, Manda. It's frightening enough without it.'

'Humbug! But, as you wish. But we'll have another go with me pushing, just so that you can try out the brakes. Here we go!' and she fastened her hands firmly against his back, and began to propel the tricycle forward with ever-increasing speed.

'Argh!' yelled Hugo again. 'It's much too fast, Manda. Slow down!' the latter being a hopeless request. Lady Amanda had no more intention of slowing down than she had of flying to the moon without the aid of a rocket.

'And away!' she cried, removing her hands and stopping, as she saw Hugo's unwilling feet relentlessly drawn to the pedals again. 'And steer round the tree, not into it, this time.' She called this last instruction after his figure, retreating down the drive at a sedate three miles an hour.

Hugo, however, did not find it sedate, and considered the idea of propelling himself, at all like this, a truly frightening experience, at his age. As a wooden bench hove into view, not far ahead of him on his current trajectory, he could hear Amanda calling to him to operate the brakes, and he clutched desperately at the two little levers below the handgrips of the handlebars.

The trike stopped, as suddenly as if it had run into a brick wall, and Hugo found himself unexpectedly flung across the handlebars, where Lady Amanda found him draped, when she caught up with him, shortly afterwards. 'What happened this time?' she asked, amazed that anyone could make such a muddle of riding a tricycle. Did he never have one as a child? she wondered.

'I pulled on the brakes, like you said, and the thing felt like the Titanic when it ran into the iceberg. It just stopped, only I didn't. Give me a hand, old thing, will you? I'm rather stuck, and need a bit of help.'

Lady Amanda obliged, and sat him gently on the bench he had nearly tried to reduce to matchwood. Having moved the tricycle to one side, she sat down beside him, and announced, 'We'll have another lesson tomorrow. I really think you're getting the hang of it now, Hugo. But before we finish for the day, let me give you one more demonstration.

'I want you to observe very closely exactly what I do, and how I do it,' she cajoled him, as she mounted the conveyance that had caused Hugo so much distress.

'Like this,' she called, looking over her shoulder at him, as she tricycled off. It was unfortunate that she was not paying sufficient attention to the direction in which she was headed. As Hugo observed as closely as he could, he suddenly observed that she had disappeared, as if swallowed by the ground itself.

'Manda, where are you?' he called, rising to his feet and beginning to totter towards the spot that she had simply ceased to occupy. 'What's happened to you? Are you all right?'

A series of strangled cries, still out of his sight, arose from a little way ahead, then Lady's Amanda's head seemed to appear from out of the ground. Hugo stopped his snail-like progress, shocked rigid by the appearance of her head, and called, 'Have you gone down a hole or something?'

'No, Hugo,' replied the erstwhile tricycling teacher, daintily spitting out the flower-head of a daisy. 'I just completely forgot about the ha-ha! Haha!'

After the application of a little iodine, and the partaking in of afternoon tea, they climbed into the Rolls to visit Enid Tweedie, to instigate her second debrief of the investigation.

They found her in a day room, socialising with other patients, and generally having a right good old time. As they entered the room, she noticed them and waved, announcing to the room at large, 'Look! Here are my friends Lady Amanda Golightly and Hugo Cholmondley-Crichton-Crump. Aren't I lucky to have such attentive friends, coming here to visit me?'

They ushered her out of the room as discreetly as possible, which meant, in Lady Amanda's case, ordering her to get on to her feet and get straight back to her quarters, so that they could have a little private chat together.

Back in her own room, Enid plonked herself into the only armchair, proprietorially, leaving her two visitors either to stand, or perch on the bed. Given their ages, they chose the latter option, and Lady Amanda began her interrogation.

'Have you found out anything more about that chap that murdered Reggie? Has Nurse Plunkett spilled any more beans?'

'She spilled a bedpan yesterday. In the corridor,' Enid informed them with glee. 'Matron gave her absolute hell for it, and she's threatened to ask for a transfer to another location. She said she could be treated like dirt at home by her family, and didn't see why she had to come here six days a week for an extra portion, considering what little she gets paid.'

'You're treating this like a visit to a holiday camp, my girl, and that won't do at all.'

'Oh, but I love it here. I'm having a very good time. I'm feeling so much better, and I'm having a really good rest. Thank you so much for arranging it for me, Lady Amanda.'

'Giving you a whale of a time wasn't the reason I booked this little visit, originally, was it, Enid? I want you here to gather information, so that we can bring a killer to justice. You're just not taking it seriously,' Lady Amanda chided her, and when you were chided by Lady Amanda, you knew about it, all right.

'But I am, my lady. Honestly! It's just that nobody else seems to have seen your chap. The time you came in visiting, when he'd not long left, is a very quiet time. It's when all the patients take an afternoon nap, so there was hardly anyone around.'

'Cunning swine! Did Nurse Plunkett know his name? We think we have it from our own investigations, but I'd like confirmation.'

'She thought he was known as 'Del', but that's all she could tell me.'

'Is she on duty this afternoon?' Lady Amanda wanted to know.

'I think so. I'll give a little buzz, and see if I can get her to come down here, so that you can ask her what you want to know yourself.'

Nurse Plunkett was available, but Matron was not happy about letting her 'socialise' with the patients. When, however, she found that this had been a special request from Lady Amanda Golightly, she capitulated. There was no way she'd win a fight with that formidable woman, and her title was the deciding factor.

'How nice to meet you, my dear,' cooed Lady Amanda, a dove of peace, for the moment. 'I wonder if there's anything more you can tell us about that chap you said they call Del?'

'I'm awfully sorry,' the little nurse replied, 'but I don't really know him. He just works for the same nursing agency that I do.'

'And which agency is that?' the cooing had become a positive purr of persuasion.

'Edwards's Nursing Agency. It's run by Malcolm Edwards,' she informed them, then Lady Amanda remembered her mobile phone, and took it out of her handbag, selected the good photograph taken by Beauchamp after the funeral, and showed it to her, saying,

'Is this the man called Del?'

'That's him. I recognised him straight off, but I really don't know anything more about him,' she replied.

'Well, thank you very much for what you have told us. You may go now.'

Nurse Plunkett seemed nonplussed by this abrupt dismissal, which was something she had not been subject to since she was at infants' school, but left the room nonetheless, feeling that to disobey might bring down, if not quite the wrath of God, then at least the wrath of Lady Amanda, and she didn't think there'd be much to choose between them. She'd heard tales of this woman's first visit to the home, and if she'd intimidated Matron, and 'sprung' one of the patients, then she was a force to be reckoned with, and not to be crossed.

Chapter Ten

The next morning, Thursday, Hugo took breakfast in bed, leaving Lady Amanda free to carry out a little errand she had been meaning to do since Hugo had moved in. She set off into what promised for now to be a fine day, on her trusty trike, for the centre of Belchester.

Travelling through the city centre on her trike was a completely different experience to going through it in the Rolls. One saw so much more, and Belchester was really a very pretty little place, if one raised one's eyes above shop frontage level. Above the sea of plate glass windows with their gaudy displays of wares, one became aware of the history of the place, and the time it had taken to grow to this wonderful mixture of styles and ages.

The latest additions to the terraces of shops had been Victorian, as the city had luckily avoided any bomb damage during the war, and these facades were typical of their era, many of them gothic revival in style. Other buildings had graceful Georgian frontages, unfussy and clean-lined. Moving back through time, one eventually encountered Tudor buildings, with their exposed beams and mullioned windows with leaded lights, above ground-floor level.

Although Lady Amanda's family had caused Belchester Towers to be built nearly two centuries ago, true Belchester families still considered the Golightlys to be incomers – Johnny-come-latelys; mere upstarts – so deeply buried were the roots of these ancient families in this very old city, which still boasted substantial and respectable remains of its venerable Roman walls.

The cathedral itself had been built to serve a living community that already possessed a considerable history, and not just to venerate and pray for the souls of the dead.

Some of the history of this long-established city could be easily read, if one only aimed one's gaze upwards, and Lady Amanda never tired of examining this mixture of architectural styles. This was not her business today, though, and she headed her tricycle for the post office: the goal of her errand.

Her business done, she headed back to Belchester Towers, encountering Hugo just exiting his bedroom, as she appeared in the entrance hall. 'Morning, Hugo,' she called cheerily. 'A bit cream-crackered after yesterday, were we?' she enquired solicitously.

''Fraid so, Manda. I'm not getting any younger, you know.'

'None of us is, Hugo. I've been into town, and I've got something here for you, that I know you need,' she replied.

'Ooh, what is it?' asked Hugo, eager to see if she had bought him a little present.

'It's a post office form to have your mail redirected to this address,' she answered, disappointing him. 'We've been collecting your post from the nursing home every time we visit Enid, but she'll be out soon, and then it'll be a real drag, so I got this form for you to fill in. If you can get it done before this afternoon, Beauchamp can drop it in for you, and Bob's your uncle.'

Hugo heaved a great sigh of despair. 'Whatever's the matter with you?' Lady Amanda enquired, surprised at his reaction. She thought he'd be pleased to get his mail organised.

'I bet it's got "full name" on it somewhere, hasn't it?'

'Of course it has, Hugo. If they didn't know that, how would they know which mail was yours for redirection?'

'I thought so.' Hugo sounded really down in the dumps.

'Whatever is your problem,' she asked, puzzled.

'Hugo Cedric Ethelred Raleigh Tennyson St John Cholmondley-Crichton-Crump,' he replied, looking downcast.

'Oh crumbs! Great-grandmother's father?' she enquired, thinking how Enid Tweedie would lap up the information that Hugo had yet another name that wasn't pronounced as it was written.

Hugo knew, without asking, that she was referring to 'St John'. 'Yes,' he intoned dolefully. Back then, ladies hadn't thought of tacking their maiden name on to the end of their husband's surname, so I got lumbered with it, as a memento of times long ago. There's been a St John in the family since Great-grandmama's day, but I shan't be carrying on the tradition, thankfully,' he explained, with a rueful smile.

'See what you mean, Hugo. Well, if you like, I'll fill it in for you, and you'll just have to sign it. What d'ya say, *compadre*?'

'I say – thank you very much. That's most civil of you, Manda. You can imagine how I've dreaded filling in forms, all my life.'

'I can, but I had no idea you were quite so encumbered! You poor sausage!' she replied, taking his arm and leading him into the drawing room.

'I never knew you'd been living only about ten miles out of the city,' commented Lady Amanda, as they sat in the morning room sipping their morning coffee. 'The last I heard, you were living in Town.'

'I came back here when I retired, then I had to go into that horrible home, courtesy of the advice of old Dr Anstruther,' he explained.

'So what happened to the family home then? It was huge, as I remember, with quite sizeable grounds.'

'Papa had to sell it after the war. That's when we moved to where I ended up. I closed the house when they died, and returned to it, as I just mentioned, when I became eligible for my pension.'

'And you never looked me up?' asked Lady Amanda.

'I thought the Golightlys would be long gone. Thought the house would probably be offices, or some sort of ghastly institution by now, and I already had problems *getting around*, and checking that out was one of the things I,' here, Hugo paused for effect, 'never *got around* to! Haha! Mild joke there, you know.'

'Very witty, old bean. You seem a lot more cheerful than when you first moved in,' commented Lady Amanda.

'I'm getting used to having company now. I must say, it was a bit of a shock to the system at first, if you don't mind me mentioning it, Manda.'

'Not at all, Hugo; and I must admit that I felt exactly the same, but it's amazing how adaptable we humans are, and how quickly we get used to new circumstances, isn't it?

'By the way, apropos your current house, I've had a few calls from estate agents who have clients who would like to view your house.'

'So long as they keep them securely locked away when they're not in use, I have no objections whatsoever. I'm quite looking forward to an increase in income, and I doubt I'll return there – oh! Was that out of order, Manda? Maybe you don't want me hanging round here long-term.'

'Of course it wasn't "out of order", as you phrase it, Hugo. I didn't expect you to go back to independent living. We seem to be jogging along all right together, and I'm sure we'll get into a way of living that allows us to have company when we want it, and a little solitude, when we feel in need of some.'

'You are a kind girl. Always were.'

'The estate agents were surprised to get the chance of letting a house the size of yours. I thought your parents were downsizing!'

'Well, you know how Mama and Papa liked to

entertain, and they thought that, although they might have lost their grand house and all its fine grounds, at least they could afford to buy somewhere where they could still entertain – weekend parties; that sort of thing – and have their friends and family to stay.'

'How very sensible of them not to buy some ghastly little bungalow on the coast and moulder away there, for the rest of their lives.'

'They had a great time for their remaining years,' Hugo informed her. 'And it was so much cheaper to run and maintain a house of that size, that they found they could entertain frequently, and, for a couple of those years, they even spent the winter in the Caribbean.'

'And now you shan't moulder away either, in some seedy little nursing home. We're going to get your knees and hips sorted out, then we're going to have some fun!' predicted Lady Amanda.

'But aren't the coffers a bit depleted?'

'Well, I act as if they are, to all and sundry. I'm doing a very good job of publicly displaying the 'mean gene' I inherited from Mummy, for I don't want people making approaches for loans or donations to whatever scrape they've got into, or for their pet charities, but no, the coffers are in very good order, but I fully intend to see that they are severely depleted, by the time I pop my clogs.'

'How did your parents manage after the war? I mean, the county was in a terrible state, and so many of the people like us just went under.'

'If you promise to keep it under your hat, Hugo, I'll tell you. But there's not another living soul knows this. Except, probably, Beauchamp. He is all-knowing and all-powerful, in his way.'

'Cross my heart and hope to die,' said Hugo, in an excited voice, and miming the actions as he spoke.

Lady Amanda lowered her voice, and whispered at him, 'Daddy was big in the black market during the war;

and, in fact until the end of rationing in the fifties. When that died out, he became an arms dealer – very hush-hush, don't yer know. But not a word of this to a living soul – not even Beauchamp, even though he knew all along what was going on. Thing is, it's just not talked about. Bad form and all that, as well as it being rather illegal, and liable to be frowned upon, even in these more liberal-minded times.'

'Good Lord! I had no idea!' Hugo was suitably shocked, right down to his pale-blue silk socks.

'Oh, don't look like that! I never had anything to do with it. I wasn't even born when all this underhand business was going on, and anyway, it all ceased when Daddy and Mummy died, but the coffers were overflowing by then, so I've just lived off what they made, ever since.'

'But how did you feel about living off money that was earned on the black market and by the sale of weapons?' Hugo asked, still suffering from the trauma of what he'd just learnt.

'I just considered that money was money. I could either own up, and hand it all over to the government, or I could spend the rest of my days in comfort, wanting for nothing, but acting much more impoverished than I am.'

'You always had the larder well-stocked, whenever we came over, and your parents never seemed to stint themselves with anything. Couldn't understand it at the time, but you never seemed to do without, like a lot of others we knew did.'

'Never had to. Daddy still got deliveries from Harrods and Fortnum & Mason's; he just arranged the delivery of their wares differently. He used to get them to deliver to a meeting place about thirty miles away, in a plain van. The deliveries were always after dark, and Daddy just drove off, collected the goods, and drove home in the Rolls. He'd just bought the car then, and was inordinately proud of it. He also left the cellars well stocked with fine wines, in the same way. Was that so wrong of us, Hugo?'

Hugo thought for several minutes, then looked up and exclaimed, 'You did exactly right! I know the black market was wrong, but, with a choice between deprivation, and an uninterrupted lifestyle, I know what I'd have chosen. Let's have some fun! I'm up for that! Is that why you didn't get requisitioned during the war?'

'Absolutely not! That was because Mummy ran a "knocking shop" for the American soldiers nearby, and that was considered to be her contribution to war work.'

Hugo actually blushed at being told this. 'Manda! How could she?'

'Oh, quite easily, as it turned out. She used the room next to yours as an office, and just approached it as she would any other business venture. Even had an extension for the telephone installed, so that she could take bookings, for the higher ranks.

'It was good money; it kept the servicemen from pestering local girls who wanted to be left alone, and it gave those who didn't the chance to earn a little extra money in very hard times. It was all, of course, kept as hush-hush as possible, the main drive never being used by either client or employees.

'There were several unofficial entrances to the grounds, and if anyone commented on the number of guests we seemed to have, we passed it off as enthusiastic entertaining. We explained the lack of vehicles by citing the shortage of petrol and coupons, and said our friends were very imaginative in their means of transport.'

'So your father was a black marketeer and a gun-runner, and your mother was a brothel-keeper?' Hugo asked, hardly able to believe what he was being told.

'That about sums it up!' said Lady Amanda, in a very matter-of-fact voice.

'You make it all sound so reasonable, Manda.' Hugo spoke in a horrified voice.

'Well, it was! It was business at its most basic level, and everyone was a winner. You can't be squeamish, when you're faced with either bankruptcy, or a little dodgy business. It was dog-eat-dog back in those days, as you well remember. We all have choices to make in life, and our way to make in the world, and, I must say, I've certainly enjoyed the benefits of my parents' ill-gotten gains, as are you, now.

'May even sell the whole bang-shoot one day, and buy a luxury villa in the Caribbean. I'd take you and Beauchamp, of course, if you wanted to come, and I'd employ some staff, so that Beauchamp can have some sort of retirement, too. I don't think I would survive very well in a dingy little flat somewhere. I'm quite at ease with myself. Does this make any difference to the way you feel about me and this place, Hugo?'

Hugo sat wreathed in silence for another few minutes, and then looked up at her again. 'Not a jot, old girl!' and he smiled. 'One can't change the past. All one can do is make the best of the present, and hope that the future is a little further away than tomorrow, and that it treats us kindly. Oh, and by the way, I'd love to come with you; warm my old bones in some Caribbean sunshine, for the rest of their days, which I hope will be many.'

'That's that, then! And remember, not a word to a living soul!'

'Be like Dad. Keep Mum!' Hugo quoted, from a wartime poster. 'Loose lips sink ships!'

They planned to go to visit Enid Tweedie again after afternoon tea, and, as usual, retired after luncheon, for their usual post-prandial naps. Hugo was first up and about again, today, and as Lady Amanda descended the stairs from her bedroom, she heard Hugo in the drawing room, singing to himself:

'Whistle while you work,

'Hitler is a berk,
'He is barmy,
'So's his army,
'Whistle while you work.'

He had a pleasant baritone voice, but seemed deeply embarrassed when she walked in on him. 'Sorry about that,' he apologised. 'Just a bit of nostalgia, after our little talk about the war, earlier, but I'm really not sure about the third line. I'm sure I haven't got the words quite right.'

'You could hardly be expected to, after all this time. After all, the war is a long time ago, and you were only ta child yourself back then - and I wasn't even a twinkle in my father's eye,' Lady Amanda commented.

'Sometimes those days seem more clear, and nearer, than yesterday. The older I get, the more I forget silly things, like what I had for lunch, or whether I've done something or not, and even where I'm going, and what I was going to fetch, when I get there.

'Memories from my childhood and youth, however, are as bright and colourful as ever. As if I could just reach out my hand and touch them.'

'It comes to us all, Hugo. It's a symptom of getting old, but the alternative's unthinkable.'

'What's that, then?'

'Dying young! Best to just trot along as we are, and get the most out of every day. Live every day as if it were your last, Hugo, because, one day, you'll be right!' she advised him, with unchallengeable common sense and logic. '*Carpe Diem*, Hugo! *Carpe Diem*! I say! Do you fancy another lesson on the old trike, before we have tea?'

'I'm not seizing anything that hard!' Hugo stated, showing a little spirit, at last.

As Lady Amanda went into the hall to collect the light jacket she would wear that afternoon, for their visit to Enid Tweedie, she found Hugo at the foot of the stairs, tapping the barometer. Again!

'Hugo!' she expostulated, 'you're always tapping at that thing. What's the fascination?'

'I've missed having my own, what with being in that place, and everything.'

'But do you have to do it, what seems like every hour, on the hour?' she chided.

'Is it really that often? I had no idea. Short-term memory and all that.'

'If you carry on like that, you'll have to do what Enid did a couple of years ago.'

'What's that?' asked Hugo, turning round in interest.

'Go into hospital and have your 'aneroids' out. That's what!' she told him, and had to stifle a snort of laughter.

Enid was still in her element, being waited on, and generally feeling like a minor member of the royal family. She had also been busy in her role as undercover agent, and had managed to get a surname out of one of the permanent members of staff who was familiar with many of the agency nurses locally.

Using the ruse that the son of a friend used to work here on a temporary basis, she made enquiries about a young man called Derek, having surmised that this was the name from which Del was derived.

Lady Amanda had already confided in her that they already had the name of one Derek Foster, but hinted that she (Lady Amanda) needed to be doubly sure, before she did anything. To have nabbed the wrong man would be unthinkably embarrassing. And on Enid's first enquiry, she had hit the jackpot.

Derek Foster, as he *was* called, had been employed there as an agency worker for only a week or so, a couple of years ago, but one particular nurse felt it her duty to recall not only past members of staff, but the names of anyone visiting the home. Recalling Derek was no problem for her, although she had not actually seen him when he had visited Reggie Pagnell.

'Must have managed to slip in when she wasn't rota-ed for duty,' guessed Lady Amanda, sitting on Enid's bed and munching distractedly on her grapes. 'Don't know how he'd found out, but he must have been very careful about when he came here.'

'The staff has quite a high turnover here,' added Enid. 'The nurse I spoke to said that there was no one here who had worked for the place for longer than eighteen months or so, except her, so he'd have no worries about being accosted by Matron, for she wouldn't know him from Adam.'

'Except for the obvious one, that she's a right old dragon.' This was Lady Amanda again, now sucking noisily on a boiled sweet, purloined from a bowl on the bedside table. 'As long as he was sure your nurse with the photographic memory was out of the way, he had a clear field in which to commit his dastardly deed,' she concluded, in a slightly muffled voice, as the sweet had decided to try to escape from her mouth, and nearly ended up on the bedspread. They could be like that, at times, boiled sweets!

'Well, at least we have a confirmed name to work with now, Manda. That's something, isn't it?' Hugo said hopefully.

'It's not the same as having an address, though, is it?' she retorted. 'How the hell do we find him with just his name? He could live anywhere. There's nothing to say that he has to live in Belchester, is there? I knew we should have followed him after the reading of the will, and not stayed behind to try to pump that old bag of wind Williams.'

There was a silence that stretched out into the eternity of three minutes, then Lady Amanda spoke again. 'I suppose there's no harm in me actually visiting the offices of Edwards's Nursing Services, posing as a client with a relative in need of care, and enquiring after a Derek Foster, whom a friend has recommended to me, as excellent?'

'That's sounds like a good ruse, Manda. You might be able to get his address from there. Who is supposed to be the patient?' asked Hugo.

'Why, you, of course, you silly sausage! Who else around here is as doddery as you are?' she asked, and received a furious scowl and a childish pout in reply.

'Will you go in disguise, Lady Amanda?' asked Enid, memories of post-war spy films flooding her memory.

'Of course not, you dolt! That sort of thing only goes undiscovered in fiction. If I put on a wig and lashings of make-up, anyone would spot at once that I was up to something dodgy. This isn't some caper film! This is real life, Enid. This chap is dangerous, and I don't want to be his next victim.'

'Who says there's going to be a next victim?' asked Hugo, now looking decidedly nervous.

'There always is, isn't there!' declared Lady Amanda. 'The first murder is the hardest, then it just gets easier and easier to kill. It's like a compulsion. Who knows how many victims there will be if we don't stop him.'

'I wish you'd stop talking about it, Manda. You're making me very anxious. He's already seen us once, at Reggie's funeral, and then we turned up at the reading of the will. If he sees us again, he's going to work out that we're on to him, somehow. I don't want him setting his mind to wiping us out, because we've worked out what he's done.'

'Never fear, Hugo! We shall come out of this unscathed, and he will be headed behind bars.'

'Thank you very much, Enid Blyton,' remarked Enid, gleefully getting her own back for what Lady Amanda had said to her just a short while ago, and Hugo offered his two-penn'orth as well.

'Eat your heart out, Agatha Christie. Now, can we get back to Belchester Towers, where I feel rather safer than out and about visiting?' he asked, acidly.

Lady Amanda's retort was curt and to the point. 'Sure can, you yellow-bellied jackal!'

That had been the nearest the two of them had come to a disagreement, and the journey home was unusually silent, both of them too embarrassed to refer to the incident. Although it had been very short, it was the sharpest exchange between them but, on entering Belchester Towers, Lady Amanda's *joie de vivre* was instantly restored, when she checked the time, and found that it was not quite five o'clock.

'There's still time to make an appointment with that chap Edwards, before the office closes,' she declared, heading for the telephone directory, with hasty steps. 'I might even be lucky enough to get an appointment tomorrow.'

Wasting not a second, she looked up the number in the Yellow Pages, and immediately dialled, without giving herself too much time to think of a story. It would be better if it was spontaneous. If she invented and rehearsed something beforehand, it would end up too complicated and convoluted, and she would forget what she had already said, and trip herself up, contradicting things she had already stated. It was much better off the cuff, then Hugo could remember for her, as he'd be listening to her end of the conversation.

Hugo eavesdropped out of necessity, as the call was answered at the other end. 'Good afternoon,' began Lady Amanda. 'I have a relative living with me who suffers mobility problems, and could do with someone visiting, maybe twice a day ... Sorry, I can't discuss this on the telephone. He might overhear.'

He was overhearing perfectly well, thank you, and had

been surprised to be referred to, firstly, as a relative, and secondly, as having mobility problems. He might be a bit slow getting around, but he was doing just fine, now he had Lady Amanda and Beauchamp to help him. He was just a bit slow: that was all.

'I wonder if I could make an appointment to come to your offices to discuss my requirements.' Lady Amanda asked, puzzled as to why Hugo seemed to be scowling at her. 'No, I don't need someone to come in as a matter of urgency; that's quite all right.' She paused, listening to the voice at the other end of the line. 'Tomorrow morning at ten-thirty? Yes, that would be very convenient. My name is Lady Amanda Golightly, and I look forward to meeting you on the morrow, to discuss my little problem,' she concluded, putting down the telephone receiver. 'Well, how was that?' she asked Hugo.

'Speaking as your "little problem" he replied, somewhat tartly, 'I don't think you should have given him your real name.'

'Horse poo, Hugo! What harm can that possibly do?'

'When you've made your enquiries about this chap Foster, it might get back to him that someone has been asking about him, and you've just given him your real name on a plate. Round here, it won't take much effort to find out that you live at Belchester Towers, with only an elderly manservant and your 'little problem' for company. Then, where will we be?'

'Don't be so melodramatic! I'm sure he's not going to come tearing round here with a gun or a machete, or even a lethal cocktail. We'll just tell the police all we've found out, hand over the "evidence" – the cocktail glass – and they'll lock him up.'

'Sez who?' asked Hugo, sarcastically. 'That inspector took no notice of you whatsoever before. Who says he's not going to do the same thing, next time you go to speak to him?'

'He won't be able to deny the evidence, when I go to see him again. He'll be compelled to take action,' she replied, somewhat huffily, as the memory of how she had been dismissed out of hand by Inspector Moody, on her previous visit, stirred in the back of her mind.

'Come along! The weather's fine and it's quite a while till cocktails. Let's go and get you on that trike again. It's about time you had another lesson,' she suggested, getting her revenge on Hugo, for his lack of faith in her powers of both detection, and persuasion.

Hugo fared a little better this time, managing both the art of pedalling, and that of using the brakes. He was tired after half an hour, but in that time, he had demonstrated that he was perfectly capable of controlling the tricycle, at very low speeds.

The next, obvious, stage, was to get him controlling the steering and brakes, with the motor running, as Lady Amanda suggested, as they walked slowly back indoors for their nightly cocktail.

'Dear Lord, Manda, give me a break! I've only just got the hang of riding the thing under my own steam. Let me get used to that, before you put a rocket in my saddlebag.'

'It's invigorating, to learn something new,' she retorted, contrarily.

'That's as may be, but not quite so invigorating, if one dies in the attempt. Let me take it at my own pace. I will manage it, but slowly-slowly. I'm not going to let you bully me on this one. You've already had me scare myself half to death on that thing, and it's just going to have to be left up to me, when I'm ready.'

'Fair enough, Hugo,' she agreed, rather meekly for her, but she was just pleased to have, sort of, got her own back on him with the trike lesson, for doubting her detection abilities. She knew she had acted pettily, and was feeling just a teensy bit ashamed of herself.

'Cocktail time, Hugo! Then din-dins! My favourite part of the day,' she said, encouragingly, and led the way into the drawing room for their daily libation.

Chapter Eleven

'Of course you can't come with me, Hugo. Don't be silly! There's no point in me explaining all about my ailing relative with mobility problems, if you're sitting beside me in his office, looking as right as ninepence, is there?'

'I don't know why he has to know I'm the supposed sick relative,' Hugo countered, sulkily.

'Because we might have to carry this charade to the point where someone visits you here, to assess your daily nursing requirements, that's why,' she explained, as if to a child.

'Oh, I see,' he replied, then added. 'I don't think I'd like someone poking and prying around my habits and abilities, let alone my body, to assess me for anything.'

'It probably won't come to that, but we must be prepared to go to any lengths necessary, to catch this chap,' she assured him. 'Just leave this one to me, and I'll do my level best to find out where he lives, from this Edwards person, this morning. If I can wheedle and smarm, and use a bit of charm, I might just come home with the goods, and we can go to visit Inspector Snooty, and give him one in the eye.'

'Might I not come in the car?' asked Hugo wistfully. 'If anything goes amiss, it might be good to have your co-conspirator around, for safety's sake?'

'I shall have Beauchamp with me, waiting in the car,' she explained airily. 'You'd better stay here out of the way, in case we need you to be the patient. If you're at all bored, you can write a narrative of our adventure so far – be a Watson to my Holmes. Dr Watson always wrote the stories, didn't he?'

'Holmes and Watson weren't real people, Manda! You really must stop living in the land of fiction,' he replied, getting another one in, on behalf of poor old Enid, yesterday, with her Hollywood-inspired spy fantasies.

'Anyway, I fancied us more as Tommy and Tuppence Beresford.'

'That couple of wet fish? Oh, Hugo, *do* set your sights higher. They were the most ghastly couple of drips who ever disgraced crime fiction!' Lady Amanda made it abundantly clear that she was not a fan.

As the front door slammed, however, Hugo reconsidered the idea of writing a Watson-esque journal, and saw that it was good. If anything happened to them, at least there would be written evidence of what they had become involved in. He also rather fancied the idea of being Watson, faithfully recording the adventures he became caught up in with his friend, Holmes.

Taking himself off to the library, he hunted out paper and writing implements, and sat down at the desk, to await inspiration for his title. After a couple of minutes chewing the end of his pen, he gave a small cry of, ''Aha!' and wrote *The Adventure of the Terminal Cocktail*, and underlined it. It might not be the best of titles, but it would do for now.

Taking up his fountain pen again, he began to write: *I find it recorded in my notebook that it was a sunny but not particularly warm day, when this matter raised its ugly head.*

At its launch I was, myself, incarcerated in a nursing home, being cared for after my old war wound had flared up again. Each day being like any other, I whiled away my time solving crossword puzzles, and wandering up and down the veranda with the aid of my trusty walking cane, smoking my faithful old pipe.

On the day in question, I had just finished reading the

110

morning paper, when a familiar old voice called out my name, and who should enter my room, but my faithful friend from childhood, Lady Amanda Golightly.

At this juncture, I had better introduce myself to the reader of my modest efforts at writing, and state that I am Hugo Cholmondley-Crichton-Crump, and have been acquainted with the Golightly family, almost since my birth. A long gap in this friendship had occurred, due to circumstances beyond the control of either party, and quite unexpectedly, I found myself re-united with the family's youngest member, Lady Amanda, still delightful, despite the passage of time.

I greeted her warmly, and rose from my prone position to shake her by the hand. Our previous relations had been warm, but formal.

Before I could utter a word of welcome, however, she raised a finger to her Cupid's bow lips, and bade me be silent, before informing me that, in a room, down the corridor, a ghastly crime had been committed. A man had been cruelly murdered.

At this point, he put down his pen, searched without success for blotting paper, and blew softly across his writing to dry the ink, before he concealed it somewhere where Lady Amanda would never find it. He'd always fancied himself a writer, but had never had the time to put pen to paper. Maybe he'd give it a try, now that he was retired, and had sufficient leisure time to do as he pleased, but he wouldn't say anything to Manda. She'd rag him terribly, and he'd die of embarrassment.

Meanwhile, Lady Amanda had a thoughtful journey to Edwards's Nursing Services, going over her cover story, so that she would be word-perfect when she got there. She had decided that, if asked what relation to her Hugo was, she'd claim him to be an older cousin, fallen upon hard times, and unable to live independently any more. She only hoped that nerves would not get the better of her and make her mind go blank – a not very 'Lady Amanda-ish' thing to happen, but then this was a first, for her.

The offices of Edwards's Nursing Services were in Snuff Street, very handy for the Birdlings Serenade prison camp, Dr Andrew's surgery and the hospital. The building that housed them was a Georgian one, its front still in original state, only a discreet brass plaque by the door identifying this as a commercial property, and not a private dwelling house.

Mounting the three steps that led up to the front door, she stepped inside to find herself confronted with a reception area with huge desk, at which sat a very efficient-looking and forbidding secretary-cum-receptionist.

'May I help you, madam?' this individual enquired, giving Lady Amanda a sharp look under her severely plucked brows.

'I have an appointment to see Mr Edwards,' Lady Amanda replied, with a confidence she no longer felt. 'It's about my cousin.' She knew she was rattled, because this was unnecessary information, and proved that she was heading towards a tendency to babble. It was an outright lie, Hugo being a relative, she decided. Just as she abhorred bad manners, thus did she feel about telling lies, too.

'Name, please?' enquired the efficient female, still giving her the once-over.

'Lady Amanda Golightly,' came the reply, and suddenly the other woman thawed, and positively purred a welcome.

So, her name still carried some weight around here. Her title was doing its job again, as it had on numerous other occasions. Lady Amanda's nerves fled whence they had come, and she began to feel her normal confident self again.

'I'll just buzz through to Mr Edwards and let him know you've arrived,' the receptionist informed her, pressing a button on an intercom service, and announcing to Mr Edwards the arrival of his client.

A voice squawked, 'Send her in, please,' its normal tones distorted by the intercom to an electronic, machine-like voice.

Malcolm Edwards's office proved to be large and luxuriously appointed. There must be a good whack to be made out of providing nursing care, Lady Amanda thought, as she lowered herself into a large comfortable armchair, across the desk from the proprietor.

'Good morning, your ladyship. How may I be of service to you?' asked Mr Edwards, and Lady Amanda immediately identified a slimy tone in his voice, indicating that he was well-versed in creeping and crawling around prospective clients, to hook them into his bank balance.

'Good morning, Mr Edwards,' she replied, then waited for him to make the next move.

'Do call me Malcolm,' he requested, and then continued, 'I believe you have a poorly relative who may be in need of the services which my humble agency is more than happy to provide,' he stated.

Yes, he was definitely an experienced crawler and shoe-licker. No need to get any coarser about the matter! 'It's my cousin,' she stated. 'He's got to an age where he's not very mobile and, although I have taken him under my wing and into my own home, I find that I am rather averse to carrying out some of the tasks with which he needs help.'

'Which are?' Golly, he was going straight for the jugular. She'd have to keep her wits about her, if she didn't want to end up employing a nurse, and not getting the opportunity to ask about Derek Foster.

'Before we go into the details, I want to state categorically that my cousin, the help needed being of the intimate sort, will only consider the services of a male nurse.'

'That's perfectly understandable, my lady.' He was in a bit of a bate himself, considering the way he attempted various ways of addressing her, evidently hoping to be directed to the correct form.

'A friend of mine has recommended a young man in your employ, whom they described as efficient, courteous and well-mannered, and I wondered if I might be able to avail myself of his services.' This was it! Make or break! She'd only get one shot at it here.

'And who might that be?' asked Mr Edwards, leaning confidentially over the desk towards her.

'I believe his name is Derek Foster,' she declared, her cards now on the table.

Mr Edwards leaned back in his chair, and adopted a rueful expression. 'I'm so sorry, Lady Golightly, but Mr Foster has just left our employ, and I am, therefore, no longer able to offer his services to you.'

Oh, goat berries! Piggy poo! thought Lady Amanda, who had just had her guns well and truly spiked. What now? she wondered. She'd have to try thinking outside the box. 'I really feel very strongly, after such a glowing recommendation from my friend, that I'd like to contact Mr Foster at home, to see if he is willing to consider coming to care for my cousin. Or perhaps he's gone to another agency?' Let's see how he liked them potatoes.

He didn't! 'I have been led to believe that Mr Foster has come into a large sum of money, and has taken advantage of this, by retiring from work altogether, and I'm afraid I cannot give out the private address of any employee, whether present or past. I do apologise for not being able to help you, but my hands are tied by the Data Protection Act. However, given the large number of nurses on my register, I'm sure we can satisfy your needs, or those of your cousin, with another male nurse. Just tell me what sort of care he is likely to need, and I'm sure I can recommend another of our staff.'

Cow poo! He had her there, and he knew it. She could tell by his face that he'd seen through her ruse, and was waiting, a slightly amused expression on his face, to see what she would do next.

'In the event of Mr Foster not being available, I feel I shall have to discuss the situation with my cousin, in light of this new information. I shall not, therefore, be able to make any decision on his behalf today. I shall go home and discuss the matter with him, and make a further appointment to speak to you, when he has made up his mind.'

She left the building with a sigh of exasperation. What a waste of time that had turned out to be. Not only would he not tell her where the rascal lived, but it would seem that he didn't work for anyone now. How had he come into money, though? she wondered. He had been left nothing in Reggie's will.

Surely he wasn't going around bumping off old people willy-nilly, after having persuaded them to change their wills in his favour. If this was so, then it hadn't happened with Reggie. Maybe Reggie had had lucid moments when he realised Foster was trying to trick him into leaving him all his money, and Foster had had to get rid of him, before he blew the gaff on his little scam – or huge scam, for all she knew. What next? she considered. She'd have to have a little think in the Rolls, on the way home.

When she returned to Belchester Towers, Hugo was still busy scribbling away in the library, enjoying himself tremendously. 'What are you up to, old bean?' she asked him, throwing her considerable bulk into a sturdy (thank goodness!) sofa.

'Writing up our adventure so far,' replied Hugo, looking up from his labours.

'I was only joking when I suggested that, you know,' she explained.

'Maybe you were, but it's jolly good fun. Ought to make a cracking yarn, once it's finished, provided, that is, that it ever does get finished, and it has a happy ending. I've really enjoyed myself while you've been gone. What about you? Any joy?'

'None whatsoever,' she told him. 'It would appear that our Mr Foster has had a large inheritance, and is no longer in paid employment. That Edwards chappie sussed out that I was fishing, and he played me like an expert. Zilch! Nowt! Nada! Although I did think on the way home, that we might just check Directory Enquiries. He must have a telephone and we've got his name. There is just a chance that they'll be able to find his telephone number for us if he lives in this area.'

'Good idea, old stick! Shall we do it now?' Hugo was getting just a little bit excited, at the thought of actually finding out where their prey's den was, so that they could beard him in it.

Lady Amanda dialled the required digits, gave the voice on the other end of the phone Derek Foster's name, then said that she didn't know his address, but it was definitely in the same telephone area as was her number.

After a short pause, there was a distant squawk from the other end of the line, and Lady Amanda's face fell so fast, it almost made a whooshing noise as it hurtled downwards. 'Thank you so much,' she intoned, in a disgusted voice, and ended the call.

'Any luck?' asked Hugo, already knowing the answer, before she told him.

'Lucked out again! He's ex-directory,' she said, with a sigh.

'Well, then we did learn something,' Hugo pointed out.

'What?' she asked. 'How? We know nothing more than we did before.'

'Yes we do, Manda. If she was looking for him, and discovered he was ex-directory, then that means he definitely lives in this area, you silly sausage.'

'So it does, Hugo! So it does! How blind I am. Why didn't I see that? But then, where does that leave us? We know he lives in this area, we know he's on the telephone, but we don't know whereabouts in this area that telephone is, and without an address, we're still stuffed, whichever way you look at it.' During this speech, her voice had gone from triumphant back to crestfallen again.

'We could always have another shot at young Mr Williams,' suggested Hugo mildly, but without hope in his voice.

'You're right again!' Lady Amanda was back in best crowing form. 'He's a very old man, and quite liable to let something slip, if he's approached in the right way. I'll ring up this afternoon, and make an appointment to see him. I can use the same excuse of wanting to try to persuade him out of early retirement for just one last case.'

'And then we could be back in business again, eh, Sherlock?' Hugo was also back on top form, at the thought that they might be able to move their investigations on again. 'Go, Manda, go! We'll nail the blackguard yet!'

After luncheon, Lady Amanda duly put a call through to Freeman, Hardy, Williams and Williams, Hugo sitting with bated breath, waiting to see if young Mr Williams would be forthcoming with the information they needed. Something, however, was not as expected, as Lady Amanda suddenly crashed down the phone and turned to look at him with an expression of absolute astonishment and horror,

'What is it, Manda? Have they been terribly rude to you?' he asked with concern.

'It's young Mr Williams!' she declared, then grabbed her handbag and made for the main hall.

'What about young Mr Williams?' called Hugo, shuffling after her, keen to be part of the action, whatever that action was.

Lady Amanda suddenly stopped, and informed him, 'He's *dead*, Hugo, and I'm going down to their offices this very minute to find out what happened. I smell a rat here, and I won't rest till I've found out where it nests!'

'Can I come?' pleaded Hugo, like a small child wanting to accompany a parent shopping.

'If you can get yourself ready and into the Rolls in two minutes flat, you're more than welcome. If my persuasive powers for information gathering prove insufficient, yours might be just the job.'

The receptionist at the legal firm's offices was crying when they arrived, but as discreetly as possible, keeping her handkerchief balled into one of her fists, when not mopping hurriedly at her eyes. The blinds on the windows facing the street were all at half-mast, as if in respect for the departed, a fitting gesture for such a long-established firm.

Hugo at once proved his worth, by approaching the receptionist, leaning down as far as he was able, mobility permitting, and put a kindly, avuncular arm around her shoulder. 'There, there, my dear,' he crooned in quiet, soothing tones. 'What ever happened to the poor gentleman?'

Having bottled up the information all morning, the secretary grabbed the opportunity to spill the beans, as a drowning man does a straw, and the dam burst open. 'They said he must have gone down to the orchard at the bottom of his garden yesterday – afternoon or evening; they're not sure which yet. He liked to sit up there in the peace and quiet, just listening to the birds, and having a drink.

'We know he sometimes took down a small jug of

Pimm's and lemonade, so that he didn't have to go back to the house to refresh his glass. He really loved it down there: said it made him forget about being old, and just put him in tune with nature. It made him happy, completely cut off from work, and not so much concerned about his own aches and pains.

'Anyway, his cleaner came in this morning, as usual, and found his bed not slept in. The first thing she did was to search the house, to see if he'd had a fall, and couldn't get up again, but there was absolutely no sign of him, so she phoned here, to see if he'd come into work, maybe having spent the night with a colleague, but, of course, he hadn't.

'Mr Freeman suggested she go out to check the garden, thinking maybe he'd collapsed or fallen out there, and might be stranded with a broken ankle or something similar, so she hung up and went to have a thorough search. She called back again after about twenty minutes, to tell us that she had found him in his usual chair in the orchard, a jug beside his chair, a glass fallen from his fingers, and that he was stone dead!'

'My dear girl,' comforted Hugo. 'What a terrible shock for you. No wonder you're upset.' As he spoke, he was aware of Lady Amanda making hideous faces at him from behind the receptionist's desk, mouthing a word. And the word was simply: 'how'?

'Has anyone any idea why he passed away so suddenly? Or had he been ill for some time, and maybe it wasn't so unexpected?' he asked, worming his way effortlessly into her confidence.

'Young Mr Williams was never ill,' she informed them. 'He was as fit as a flea, and we quite confidently expected him to live long enough to receive a letter from Her Majesty. That was why it was so shocking.' Her valiant effort to unburden herself of this information suddenly faltered, and she raised her handkerchief to her eyes again, as a flood of fresh tears overwhelmed her.

'And there's going to be an inquest and everything, because he hadn't seen a doctor for so long. Oh, the shame, and they won't even let the poor old man rest in peace. They're going to cut him about, and do all sorts of undignified things to him which he would have hated, were he alive. It seems so obscene, to subject him to that, even after death.'

'There, there, don't fret. Young Mr Williams is at peace now, and nobody can insult his dignity. He's beyond earthly interference, and with his God.' Hugo did feel a bit two-faced about this, as he had ceased to believe in the Superior Being many years ago, but it seemed to have had a soothing effect on the woman.

'You're right, of course!' she said, blowing her noise loudly, in a most unladylike and indiscreet way. 'I know what you say is true. It's just the shock, you know? It's left me feeling thoroughly rattled, and now I'm neglecting my duties to the firm. What can I help you with? You must have come in here for a reason.'

It was Lady Amanda's turn, now, to be inventive. Smiling as sweetly as she could manage, she plonked herself in front of the desk, and said, 'It's nothing that can't wait, my dear girl. We'll take ourselves off, in the light of the loss you have all suffered, and come back another time, when circumstances aren't quite so trying. Don't give it another thought.'

Once more outside and out of hearing, she took Hugo's arm, and declared, 'Well, I'll be! What a couple of Am-Dram sleuths we're turning out to be, eh? Perfect team, and all that! You did a marvellous job of getting her to spill the beans. I'd just have sailed in there and demanded to know what was going on, and got the old bum's rush, but you charmed it out of her, and at the same time, made her feel better.'

'You had your part to play, too,' Hugo replied. 'If it

hadn't been for your get-up-and-go, we'd never have gone there in the first place. You didn't waste a minute, after you were told on the phone that there had been a death. You just got on with tracking the matter down to its hub.'

'Thank you, so much, Hugo. Ah, there's Beauchamp, with the Rolls. He has been lucky with the parking today.'

'It hasn't got us any further, though, with finding out where Foster lives, has it?' Hugo asked, suddenly downcast again, as he remembered the real reason they had contacted the legal firm. 'And with the old man gone, it looks like a dead-end for us, don't you think?'

'Not necessarily,' replied Lady Amanda, then made a noise that sounded very like 'ping'.

'Whatever's up with you, Manda? Do you need basting, or something?' This was Hugo's attempt to alleviate the mood of gloom that had settled over him.

'What a pair of dolts we've been!' she suddenly exclaimed, her face breaking out into a broad grin. 'Register of Electors,' she declared. 'We must go to the library at once! That's where we'll learn what we need to know.'

'Can't we leave that till tomorrow?' begged Hugo, whose limited store of energy had just registered empty.

'All right! But, first thing, mind you. Sparrow fart! Stupid o'clock! We want to be there as the library opens, and not nearly lunchtime. Agreed?'

'Agreed!' concurred Hugo, with a sigh of relief.

Chapter Twelve

At breakfast the next morning, Lady Amanda stated, 'I bet there was something in that jug of Pimm's, or in his glass.'

'You think it's the same chappie, killing again?' enquired Hugo.

'I do,' she assured him. 'I'll bet they discover enough poison in his system to have killed a herd of elephants. Our young Mr Williams may have spotted something odd, put two and two together, and unknowingly signed his own death warrant.'

'How?' asked Hugo briefly, his mouth still half-full of scrambled egg.

'He knew, as we do, that that young chap was somehow mixed up in Reggie's affairs. We also know that this Del was left hardly anything in the will, but still attended both the funeral, and the wake, with the reading of the will. I wonder how he explained his presence to young Mr Williams. Why should someone, who hadn't nursed the deceased for some time, be interested in attending his funeral, especially as there was nothing in it for him?'

She paused for a few seconds. 'What if he got wind that Foster had been posing as Reggie's nephew, at the home? I mean, it's quite likely, isn't it, if young Mr Williams went to take possession of Reggie's bits and pieces, him having no living relatives, that someone might have said something to him about how nice it was, that Reggie's nephew got in touch with him again, just a few months before he died?

'In fact, I remember hailing him as Reggie's nephew, at

Reggie's house. I wonder if young Mr Williams overheard, and became suspicious about Foster? Lord! Then, it could've been me who got him killed. What a ghastly thought! But I do think this was done by the same hand. The modus operandi is the same.'

'You've got a point there, Manda.'

'And if Mr Williams mentioned something, or questioned Foster about it, he would definitely have put himself in danger, wouldn't he?'

'By George! I think she's got it!' exclaimed Hugo, unconsciously echoing words from *Pygmalion*. 'We've got to bring this bounder to justice!'

'Quite right! He's killed twice now, and he won't hesitate to kill again.'

'I rather think you ought to go and speak to that policeman again, Manda. This is getting very dangerous.' Hugo's concern for her safety shone out through his eyes, and behind that was discernible a deep concern for his own safety, as well.

'Tommyrot!' she exploded, showering the table with toast crumbs. 'What, go to that man and be humiliated again? Be treated as a batty old lady who has delusions? I won't, I say! We'll wrap this up ourselves, and then hand it to him on a plate, and watch his embarrassment, as he realises that I was right all along; that's what we'll do.'

'Well, we'd better go carefully. I'm quite happy with my cashmere overcoat, and don't want to be measured for a wooden one, anytime soon. We'll need to tread very carefully. I know the word 'carefully' is probably not in your vocabulary, Manda, so I suggest you go and look it up in a dictionary, after breakfast.'

'Cow poo, Hugo! Doggy doodles! He who dares, wins!' she retorted emphatically.

'As long as it's not "he who dares, dies"!' was Hugo's somewhat waspish reply.

Finding an address at the library for Derek Foster took quite some time, but nowhere as near as long as it could have taken, had they not had a stroke of luck. Lady Amanda had decided that, if they looked at the Belchester map, they could look at the relative positions of the nursing home, Edwards's Nursing Services, and the address of the residual legatee of Reggie's will. As she pointed out to Hugo, he wouldn't want to be too far away from either place, if all this was pre-meditated.

Unfortunately, although Lady Amanda had made a note of the name and address of the main beneficiary of the will, she had carelessly written it down on an old envelope she had found lurking in her handbag, and she had cleared out said handbag, only the night before, as it was getting rather full with things like apple-corers, screwdrivers, tape measures, corkscrews and the like. The envelope would now be residing in the waste paper basket in the drawing room.

'Thank goodness Beauchamp won't empty it, this being his nominal day off, when he does nothing that isn't absolutely necessary,' she said. 'Let's note down the street names that are possible, taking into account the other locations, and see if we're fortunate enough to come up with anything.'

They sat themselves at one of the library tables, and began their search; the next two hours being filled with such comments as: 'I didn't know he was still around' 'I thought he'd moved away' and 'I could have sworn she was dead'. It may have been tedious, but, in some ways, it was a little like a walk down memory lane.

'I say, guess who's moved into that big house near the cathedral', 'I never thought his son would leave home'. They carried on in this manner until the librarian himself came over, and asked them, please, to observe the rule of silence, and they hunted on with only the odd squeak of recognition, as they came across familiar names from times gone by.

It was half-past lunchtime, when Hugo made a *sotto voce* exclamation of triumph. 'Got the wretch!' he whispered across the table to Lady Amanda. 'I'll just make a note of the address, then we can get out of here, and go and get something to eat. I'm starving!'

An extremely loud and long drawn out 'Shhhhhh!' carried across from the desk to their table, the sibilance alerting other users of the reference area, that someone was in trouble, so, putting away their notepads and pens, they gathered themselves together and made as dignified an exit as they could manage, under the stern and disapproving eye of the librarian, who was thoroughly fed up with them.

They were worse than the children that came in, in his opinion, and he was glad to see them leave, at last. His haven of tranquillity had been invaded, for over three hours now, by those two inconsiderate bodies, and he hoped they didn't intend returning in the near future.

Once outside, Lady Amanda did her level best to jump up and down with glee, but with only a modicum of success, given her age and weight, and Hugo, who understood how victorious she felt, simply nodded his head vigorously, in agreement with the sentiment.

Before she could speak, however, he pre-interrupted her. 'No, Manda! Not today! We have to plan this carefully. Our lives could be at stake.'

'Well, at least we can discuss it when we get home,' she replied, her bottom lip stuck out in disappointment.

'We can discuss it as much as you like, but we mustn't rush into anything perilous. As there's probably not a lot of it left for me, I find myself very fond of life. I'd hate to do anything that would hasten its end, and I'm sure you feel the same way.'

'Spoil sport!' she retorted, sticking out her tongue at him in frustration and defiance.

'We'll tackle this with the greatest of caution, or not at

all!' declared Hugo, standing his ground, and feeling the very first traces of the development of a backbone. 'Now, let's find the Rolls and get back for lunch. My stomach thinks my throat's cut!'

Given that all three of them had arrived home well past the usual hour for luncheon, and that it was, technically, Beauchamp's day off (he had already driven them to the library and back) the manservant did a pretty slick job of serving them a simple lunch, with the minimum of fuss or delay.

'Now you see why, if I do decide to sell the lot, and beetle off to the Caribbean, I'd take Beauchamp with me. Apart from the fact that he's worked here all his working life, I'm so used to him now, that I feel I really couldn't manage without him.' Lady Amanda was purposefully avoiding the subject of what their next actions should be, with regard to hunting down this double murderer.

However, it wasn't so easy to pull the wool over Hugo's eyes as she thought, and he pierced her with a steely gaze, and said, in as commanding a voice as he could summon, 'I know what you're up to, and it won't work!'

'I'm not up to anything, Hugo. Whatever do you mean?' she asked, innocently, but not fooling her old friend for a minute.

'I know you, of old,' he stated. 'And I'm going to keep an eagle eye on you, for the rest of the day. If I catch you sneaking off anywhere on your own, you'll have me to answer to. You're not young and fit any more, you're old and vulnerable, and you'd better wise up to that fact, now. I don't want you taking any unnecessary risks. After all, if anything happened to you, where should I live?'

This last, apparently selfish question, he had asked with the idea of goading her out of her habitual recklessness, and bringing her back down to earth, by making her think of someone else's welfare, for a change, and not just the opportunity (and risk) of covering herself with glory. It was all very well, her wanting to show up that inspector, but not at the expense of her own life. That would be a hollow victory, indeed.

She sighed. 'You're a fussy old woman, Hugo, but you do have a point. I promise to do nothing without consulting you first. OK?'

'Show me your hands, Manda,' he ordered, scrutinising them minutely, when she held them out for his inspection. As she looked at him quizzically, he added, 'Just checking, to see that your fingers weren't crossed!'

At that point, Hugo toddled slowly off to 'wash his hands'. Giving him sufficient time to reach his destination, Lady Amanda uncrossed her toes (sneaky old baggage that she was) and made her way to the wastepaper basket, where she retrieved the discarded envelope with the name written on it, scanned it briefly, and slipped it back into her handbag, where she could access it easily.

After their meal, Lady Amanda settled innocently in the drawing room with the local paper, which was never delivered to Belchester Towers until the day after it was published. As was her habit, after scanning the front page, she turned straight to the announcements to see who had been hatched, matched, or despatched. Her eyes devoured the columns eagerly, until she came to one entry, which made her shout out in surprise.

'Whatever is it, old girl?' asked Hugo, who was wandering through his copy of the *Daily Telegraph* without much interest. 'Been bitten by something?'

'It's in the *Deaths* column!' she nearly shouted. 'We've got the rotter!'

'What's in the *Deaths* column?' asked Hugo, wondering whose passing could have elicited such excitement from her.

128

'*Richard Churchill Myers of six Wilmington Crescent, Belchester, died peacefully in his sleep* – let me see, ah! – *Thursday night, at home, after a long illness. Will be missed by his loving nephew, Derek Foster.* That was the day after the will reading! The evil little beast!'

'Whatever are you on about, Manda? At least he was someone's nephew.' Hugo still hadn't quite caught up with events.

'Myers!' she declared. That was the name of the chap who inherited the bulk of Reggie's estate. It says in here that he's just died, and his nephew's only *our* chappie, who seems to like eliminating anyone who gets in his way, concerning his acquisition of money.'

'And you think he murdered his real uncle, too?'

'Of course he did! It's as plain as the nose on your face. First he bumps off Reggie, so that his estate goes to this Myers chap, Foster's uncle, then he does away with this uncle, who's probably not got any other relatives, if his nephew posted the death notice. And, in between, poor young Mr Williams gets wiped out. He probably only got a whiff of what was going on, and tackled him, in all innocence, about it.'

'Well, I never,' exclaimed Hugo. 'We've got him! Can't we just hand him over to the police now?'

'Over my dead body!' said Lady Amanda.

'That's rather what I'm worried about,' parried Hugo. 'Just report him, and leave it at that.'

'But there's not enough evidence. I can see exactly what happened, now. I reckon he was nursing old Reggie at home, until he went a bit gaga. I surmise that Reggie and that Myers chap must once have been good friends, and we know Reggie had no relatives to leave anything to, so he must have made his will in this old friend's favour.'

'This is all surmise, you know. You may be completely wrong,' Hugo said, hoping to temper her enthusiasm with a little common sense.

'Rot, Hugo! You know I'm right!' She rolled right over him like a verbal steamroller, and continued, 'If this blighter nursed Reggie, he'd probably have found out that he was leaving a bundle to his uncle, who was probably already ill – it says here: after a long illness.

'Well, what if his uncle took a turn for the worse, and he thought Reggie would probably outlive him. He'd need to do something about that, wouldn't he? And what better action to take, for his own evil purposes, than to remove Reggie from the equation? The money would then go to his uncle without question, uncle dies, and Bob's your uncle – sorry about that! – and Foster would cop for the lot.

'The only fly in the ointment was young Mr Williams, who smelled a rat, so he had to be removed as well. For all we know, Foster might have hurried his uncle into the next world as well, getting impatient to be a relatively rich man, leading a life of leisure.'

'Why don't you just tell all this to that Inspector Moody, Manda, and let him do the sniffing around?' asked Hugo, demonstrating that he, at least, had some common sense left.

'Because nobody but us, and presumably young Mr Williams, suspected anything in the first place. It was only because I found that cocktail glass in Reggie's room, and smelled the spilt stuff on the floor, that I thought there was something fishy about his death. As far as the law's concerned, Reggie died a natural, peaceful death; young Mr Williams just slipped away due to his age; and the Myers chap, having been ill for a long time, won't even have a post mortem.

There'll be no trouble with the death certificate, because he'd had a long illness: probably cancer – it usually is, these days. So they'll just cremate him, probably; the same with young Mr Williams, and nobody will ever be any the wiser, if we don't do something about it. You remember what Williams said about Foster – that he wanted Reggie cremated, and not buried, but – thank God – he was buried, so we could still force an exhumation.'

'Aren't you running just a bit ahead of yourself there, Manda?' asked Hugo.

'I don't think so, Hugo. Somebody's got to sort out this mess, and it might as well be us. Nobody else is interested, and until we can provide adequate evidence that crimes have been committed, nobody will listen to us.'

Hugo managed to keep Lady Amanda in check by suggesting that she give him another lesson in taming the trike, and this distracted her for a while, but during afternoon tea, she was back at the 'trouser leg' of the murders again, like a Jack Russell with a rat.

'You never actually gave me the address, did you, Hugo, old boy?' she pumped him, like a car nearly out of petrol and desperate for fuel.

'What address is that, then, Manda?' he replied, playing the innocent.

'You know darned well what address I'm talking about. Don't be obtuse,' she retorted, a growl creeping into her voice.

'The address of my house for the estate agents?' he asked, without hope, but more as a distraction and time-waster.

'The address of that Derek Foster that you found this morning.' Anger was making her sound like a furious cat, disturbed at its food.

'Can't seem to remember where I wrote it down,' Hugo parried, knowing he wouldn't win, but hoping he might distract her sufficiently so that she was put in a foul enough temper to forget what her original purpose had been.

'You wrote it in the little section at the back of your

diary, where you always make notes. You haven't forgotten at all. You're just doing this to rile me.'

'It's working then!' Hugo commented, noticing the rise in the pitch of her voice as he continued to prevaricate.

'Hugo!' she shouted. 'Give me that blasted address!'

'All right! Keep your hair on.' Reaching into his trouser pocket, he produced his diary, flicked to the back pages, where he made a note of anything he particularly wanted to remember, and read: 'Eleven, Mogs End, Belchester. That's to the south of the city, isn't it?'

'Yes. It runs off Lumpen Lane, cutting through to Rag-a-Bone Road. It's only a sort of alley, really, and the houses are just a few tumbledown old cottages; should have been condemned and demolished years ago, in my opinion, but then who am I to contradict the nosy-parker preservation societies that seem to proliferate today?'

'Satisfied now?' he asked, putting away his diary.

'Absolutely! We'll go tonight!'

'What do you mean, we'll go tonight? Go where? Why? This all sounds a bit iffy to me.'

'We'll go and scout out the house – make sure he lives there – that sort of thing. It's only a little tidying up. We need to be absolutely sure of our facts, before we can take this investigation any further,' she explained, in the most rational of voices, as if it were perfectly normal to go skulking about at night, trying to see into people's homes, before getting them arrested for what was now triple murder.

'Manda! You can't be serious! What if he catches us – you? I'm certainly not going peering through folks' windows, spying on them in their own homes.'

'I shall pretend to be an old lady who has come over queer, and would like a glass of water – something of that order should do it,' she informed him, without a hint of embarrassment.

'But he'll recognise you!' Hugo warned. 'What do you

do, then, when he confronts you with being at Reggie's funeral, the wake, and the reading of the will?'

'I shall go in disguise,' she retorted, giving him a scornful look, as if this were so obvious that he should have thought of it himself. She seemed completely to have forgotten how she had poured contumely on this idea, when Enid had suggested it.

'You can't!' expostulated Hugo, in as masterful a voice as he could manage.

'I can, Hugo. And what's more, I will. There are no street lights down that alley, and it should be easy enough to sneak into the garden and look through a lighted window – much easier after dark than in broad daylight.' Lady Amanda had made up her mind, and nothing in the world would make her change it.

'Well, how are you going to get there?' Hugo asked. 'Surely not on that tricycle of yours? There's no way you could make an effective escape on that. He'd catch you in no time.'

'I shall get Beauchamp to take us – us, you notice, in case I need your help – in the Rolls, and park it in Lumpen Lane. There's a tiny piece of waste ground at the junction with Mogs End where Beauchamp can park, and extinguish the car lights. No one will notice it there.'

'I don't see what sort of help you think I could be to you. I'm hardly up for a sprint escape, or for wrestling with villains.'

'You could call the police if anything happened to me; if I didn't come back, or something.'

'Oh, great! So I have to sit inside a pitch-black car, waiting for something dreadful to befall you, before I'm of any use. Beauchamp would be a lot handier than me.'

'Fact is, Hugo, I want you to be there. This is our adventure, and I don't want you to miss out on any of the fun,' she explained.

'Fun?' Hugo was astonished by this view of what they

were proposing to do. 'I'm going to speak to Beauchamp,' he threatened. 'I shall forbid him to drive you anywhere tonight after dark.'

'Surely you don't want to force me to carry out this necessary surveillance with the tricycle as my only conveyance and means of escape, do you?'

'Manda, that's not fair. Of course I don't. If you must carry out this hare-brained scheme, then of course I'll accompany you, even though the thought of it worries me to death.'

'Good man, Hugo! That's the spirit!' She was always magnanimous in victory. Getting her own way bucked her up no end.

Chapter Thirteen

It wasn't dark enough for them to leave until half past nine, and it took a further twenty minutes to get Hugo out of the house and into the car. First he had had to go to the lavatory, then he had decided that he really ought to take a light jacket against the cool of the evening, then he claimed to have left his glasses in his bedroom.

When he stated that he had to go to the lavatory again, as anxiety always affected his bladder, Lady Amanda decided that this was the last straw, and rushed him from the cloakroom, through the front entrance, and into the car. She would brook no more shilly-shallying and time-wasting, and put her foot down with a firm hand [!]

The drive through Belchester at this time of night was very pleasant. Not being a great centre for night clubs and partying, the few public houses the city did possess were usually frequented by older residents who wanted only a quiet drink. Those who wanted a more riotous time left the city for other destinations with more glittering establishments on offer.

The little city was almost deserted and, with its street lights in the style of Victorian gas lights, charmed anew, with this slip back in time, and its unpopulated streets. Beauchamp turned right, out of North Street in to West Street, then took the first turning left, into a road called simply and accurately West-to-South, then first right into Lumpen Lane, which was shaped like the letter 'U'.

At the bottom of its curve was a right-hand turn into Mogs End, and, opposite this junction, a small piece of ground, unused since a venerable cottage had been demolished due to its unsafe structure; a victim of neglect and lack of care.

Beauchamp drew the car to a halt on this tiny piece of waste ground, handed a torch back to Lady Amanda, then extinguished the car's lights. 'Take care of yourself, my lady,' he mumbled, as he handed it over, and Hugo leaned across to Lady Amanda and whispered, 'Keep your eyes peeled, old girl, and never underestimate the power of a scream.

'If we hear anything of you, Beauchamp can rush to your aid, and I can get in the front and lean on the horn, until everybody living hereabouts comes outside, to see what all the noise is about.'

'Hugo?' she hissed back.

'Yes?'

'Why are we whispering?'

'I haven't the faintest idea, Manda. It just seems appropriate, somehow.'

Lady Amanda slipped from the car, with absolutely none of the grace and elegance of a cat, and immediately caught her toe on a half brick, causing her to exclaim, audibly, in surprise and pain, an action that drew an even louder 'shh' in stereo from the Rolls.

'I'm OK,' she hissed back. 'I'll just put my torch on for a minute, until my eyes get more used to the low light.' There may not have been any street lighting in Mogs End, but it was a clear night, and the sky provided sufficient illumination for her, after just a few steps.

Trying to act as normally as possible, she extinguished her torch and put it in her pocket before starting to saunter down Mogs End, keeping as keen an eye out as she could, in the low visibility, for the house numbers. She was not sure which end the numbering began, nor which side had the odd numbers, and which evens.

She was on the right-hand side of the street, as one approached it from this end, and the second house had, fortunately for her, a large number '4' on its gate, so at least she had the information required, to locate number eleven. The numbers obviously started at this end, and the odd numbered cottages were on the other side of the road.

Looking around her with a nonchalance she did not feel, she crossed the road and began to stroll slowly past the cottages with the odd numbers, counting as she went. 'I must have passed one and three, so, five next, seven – no lights on in there at all, they must be out – nine, television blaring, and *there* – number eleven.'

She whispered to herself to boost her confidence, because, at this very moment, she felt uncharacteristically frightened. Anything could happen to her, going into enemy territory like this. She'd brushed and sprayed her hair flat, worn her tattiest old gardening clothes, and smeared on some very bright make-up, before leaving home, but she suddenly felt naked – exposed as she never had been before, and as if she had a name card round her neck, confirming her identity to all and sundry.

At the garden gate, she paused, and looked over it to see how it opened, undid the bolt with the greatest of care, and then froze on the spot. What if he had a dog? It would come rushing at her a soon as she set foot on the property, barking its head off. What if it was a large dog? A vicious dog?

Scolding herself for such cowardice, she grabbed the gate and began to open it very slowly, stopping after only about six inches, because it was badly in need of oiling, and screeched like the very devil itself. A light came on in the front room of the house, and she ducked down into a crouching position as quickly as she could manage, behind the hedge that fronted the property. It was quite a height, and very unkempt, and made a good shield for someone of her bulk.

The front door was opened, and a voice called, 'Is there anyone there?' It was Foster's voice, all right. She was definitely at the right place, but this was no consolation, now that he had become aware of her presence. Or had he? He might just put it down to not having shut the gate properly.

She was right. A few footsteps sounded on the very short garden path, and the gate was kicked shut. This was a blessing, as Foster never got as far as actually taking a look out into the street. She'd just have to get in some other way.

When the front door had slammed shut, she crawled along the very narrow pavement, eventually finding a place where there had been a gap in the hedge, and it would be possible for her to swarm her way through, even though the hedge was in the process of managing this breach in its defences. So much for being discreet, she thought. If any of the neighbours were to come out of their houses, she would look like an old soak, crawling home after a binge!

It was no easy job, penetrating that hedge, even though it grew much more sparsely at her point of entry. Twigs and branches caught at her hair and her clothing, and nettles stung at her ankles as she scrambled her way through. One wayward frond of foliage found its way up her skirt in the most undignified way, and assaulted her most viciously, in a place for which she could not possibly seek sympathy. But she was determined to get to the other side, finally reaching it on all fours, and having to put her hand back through it for her hat, which had been whipped off, and deposited back on the narrow paving, on the other side.

Gathering her dignity as best she could, she stayed in her prone position, and approached the side of the house, still on all fours. The light at the front of the house had been switched off again, but there was a light to the right-hand side, which she considered might possibly be the kitchen, as the starlight revealed pipes exiting the wall, and disappearing into what she supposed was a drain.

On reaching the window from which the light illuminated an oblong of the garden, she slowly slid into an upright position – it had to be slow. Fast, she couldn't do, at her age – and pressed herself against the wall of the property. Maybe, if she was very careful, she could sneak a peek into the interior.

She had no idea what she expected to achieve by this action, she suddenly realised, and all the adrenalin, which had buoyed her up thus far, suddenly evaporated, leaving her feeling old and foolish. What had she hoped to achieve by this nocturnal reconnaissance visit? Well, it was no good making a bolt for it now. She'd just have to achieve what she had set out to achieve, and get a look into this chappie's house.

The feeling of foolishness continued to nag at her. Had she really expected to find him brewing some sort of devilish potion in his kitchen, intent on claiming the lives of more victims? What was she playing at, and at her age, too? She ought to be ashamed of herself, but that would have needed a grown-up attitude, and she never intended to grow up properly.

Dismissing such negativity from her mind, she remembered that the Golightlys weren't quitters, and she steeled herself to lean round, as rapidly as she could, and sneak a peek into that kitchen. She bunched her muscles, drew in a large breath, which she held, with the suspense of the moment, and bobbed her face rapidly across the window pane, and back again.

There had been nobody in the room. It was empty. Thus emboldened, she took a more leisurely look at the interior of the room, looking for goodness knows what, but alert to any alien item, out of place in such an environment.

As she committed the contents of the room to memory, she became aware of a low, menacing growling, which seemed to be coming from just behind her slightly crouched figure. The hairs on the back of her neck began to rise, and she turned, very slowly, to see just what was to her rear.

As she began to move, the growling turned to a deep baying bark, and a voice ordered her to stay where she was. Completing her one-hundred-and-eighty degree turn, she found herself almost nose to nose with a dog she immediately identified as a Great Dane, its collar held in a firm grip by its owner, Derek Foster.

'Don't move or cry out,' he commanded. 'I've phoned the police and they're on their way. I suggest you just stay where you are until they arrive, unless you'd like to take on Marmaduke here.'

'I'll stay,' she whispered, and gradually straightened up, until she was in a more comfortable position. The dog growled again, and gave two mighty 'wuffs'.

'I also suggest you keep quiet. Marmaduke doesn't take kindly to strangers.' After a few seconds of silence, he asked, 'Aren't you that woman who came to my father's friend's funeral? You can talk now I've spoken in an ordinary social voice. He won't make a move if I act in a civilised fashion towards you.'

'I was there, yes.'

'Why?' he enquired, still speaking softly.

'Because Reggie was an old friend, and an ex-business partner of my father's. I was just paying my respects.'

'Is that all?' He sure was nosy, she thought.

'Of course!'

'Then why did you stay on after the wake, for the reading of the will? Hoped he'd left you something, was it?'

'Something like that,' Lady Amanda agreed, not sure where this conversation was leading, but not enjoying it one little bit.

At that moment, what she considered to be their sinister

little exchange of un-pleasantries was interrupted by the wail of a siren, and a police car drew up in the road outside the cottage, its lights providing a bright show of red and blue, but that was not all. A Rolls-Royce approached from the other direction, and also parked, nose to nose with that belonging to the forces of law and order.

'Thank God!' Lady Amanda muttered, her voice drowned by the still unquenched wails of the siren. 'Beauchamp has ridden to my rescue!' and her whole body relaxed, shortening her height by a good two inches, and decreasing the pressure in her bladder, which had grown considerably, during her little conversation with Foster and his hell-hound.

At the gate, Beauchamp was standing aside courteously, to allow a uniformed policeman and one in plainclothes to precede him, and all three figures approached the tableau presented by an elderly lady slumped against the side wall of the cottage, and a man, responsibly restraining a large and angry dog.

'Shall we go inside?' enquired the policeman not in uniform, and Lady Amanda's spirits slumped to new depths. It was that Inspector Moody, who already suspected her of being batty. How was she going to talk herself out of this situation, without confirming his original suspicion?

Once inside the cottage, Beauchamp took over with his usual aplomb, and confirmed, without a shadow of a doubt, that Lady Amanda had bats in the belfry. 'I am Lady Amanda's family retainer,' he explained. 'She often goes wandering,' he continued, in a perfectly reasonable tone. 'It runs in the family. There's many a time, in the past, when I've had to locate her late mother, out for one of her little jaunts, looking through other people's windows, to see how the other half lives.

'She's not dangerous: just wants to watch other people

getting on with their lives, in homes so different from her own. If I could only persuade her to get a television set, it would probably solve the problem instantly with, perhaps, an addiction to *Coronation Street*, or one of the other soap operas, that I believe are on offer, these days.

'But she is adamant that she won't have such a thing as a television in the house, and this is the result. Please accept my sincere and humble apologies, and be assured that I will keep a closer eye on her in the future, if she's in one of her exploring moods.'

Moody looked at the dignified figure of the manservant thoughtfully, considering whether he was telling the truth, or just trying to talk his employer out of an awkward situation. After a short silence, he gave Beauchamp the benefit of the doubt, having been subjected to Lady Amanda's visit to the police station, and her ramblings about there having been a murder committed at a local nursing home.

'I sympathise with your predicament,' he intoned, addressing Beauchamp for the first time. 'Do you have transport to get the old lady home safe and sound?'

'I do, indeed, Inspector. The family Rolls-Royce is parked outside, awaiting us for the journey home, if you will be so generous as to permit us to leave.'

Moody thought about it, but had one or two more questions. 'And you'll definitely keep a sharper eye on her in future?'

'Certainly, Inspector,' replied Beauchamp with dignity.

'And do you know how she got here tonight?'

'I strongly suspect it was by tricycle,' he answered, making the inspector gape with surprise. 'No doubt on the route home, I shall find it abandoned somewhere, and simply come back to collect it with the trailer, when I have got my charge settled for the night.'

It all seemed perfectly reasonable to Inspector Moody, who had been convinced, since his first encounter with

Lady Amanda, that she was as daft as a brush. Being *Lady* Amanda, probably just meant that the family could afford to pay for a 'minder' for her, rather than put her in a home for old crazies, which is where he, personally, considered she should be.

'I shall release her into your care, then. But I shall be keeping an eye out for her in future. We can't have batty old biddies going around giving people terrible shocks, like that which she inflicted on Mr Foster this evening.'

'You have my guarantee, Inspector,' said Beauchamp, pulling himself up to his full dignified height, and glaring at Lady Amanda, with the command to stay absolutely silent, in his eyes. She was getting agitated, and if she spoke now, it would ruin everything.

'In that case, you may take her away. Trespass is a civil offence, and I understand that no damage has been done. Do you want to press charges for anything, Mr Foster?' he asked.

'No. I just want her to leave me alone,' replied the householder.

'That's good enough for me,' stated the inspector. 'You are to stay away from this gentleman's house – in fact from any house, the windows of which you might want to peer through, indiscriminately. Do you understand me?' he asked, piercing Lady Amanda with his steely gaze.

She made as if to speak, but Beauchamp reached out a foot at the speed of lightning, and trod on her toes. 'Ahhh!' she cried and, getting the message that had been so painfully delivered to her, added, 'I understand.'

'Good!' replied Inspector Moody, not having noticed Beauchamp's swift and effective action. 'I do not expect to run into you again in similar circumstances. Do I make myself perfectly clear to you?'

'Yes, Inspector.'

'You may take her home, now, Mr Beauchamp. And you'd better make sure she stays there, and doesn't go off on one of her little "peeping-tom jaunts" again, or she'll be for it.' Turning to the uniformed officer who had driven him there, he instructed him, 'I want you to keep an eye out for this old lady. She can be a real nuisance. Got that, Constable Glenister?'

'Got it, sir,' replied the navy-blue clad figure, trying his hardest to suppress a smile at the situation. 'If I see her, I'll run her in, and deliver her straight to you, Inspector.'

'Good man!' Turning now to Lady Amanda and Beauchamp, he advised them to be on their way, and to keep under his radar, in the future.

Lady Amanda was speechless with rage, as they walked over to the Rolls, and then speechless with fury when she found Hugo lying across the backseat of the vehicle, snoring away as if he hadn't a care in the world.

'Hugo!' she yelled, then pushed his leaden body as far as she could across the seat, so that she could get into the car herself. 'There I was, in danger of my life, held at bay by a slavering monster of a dog, and then the police arrived.'

'Wossat?' slurred Hugo, endeavouring to pull his sleep-drugged old body into an upright position.

'And it wasn't just any old policeman,' she continued, ignoring the dilapidated state in which he had found himself, at being woken suddenly. 'Oh no, it was Inspector Moody – the charming and polite Inspector Moody!'

'And then what happened?' asked Hugo, his wits reassembling themselves with surprising speed.

'*Then* Beauchamp came along and explained to the kind inspector that I was a loopy old biddy, who couldn't be trusted out on her own. And very convincing he was too, weren't you Beauchamp?'

The sound of a murmured, 'Beecham,' reached them from the driver's seat.

'So now he's had his worst fears confirmed, and he's

even asked his constable – one PC Glenister, I believe – to keep his eyes peeled for me, in case I go wandering off again, to try to spy through people's windows, and watch them watching television, and doing other equally exciting things. And that brute with the dog! Why didn't he say anything about coming across us before? That's very suspicious behaviour in my opinion.'

'Cor lummy, Manda! You did get yourself into a pickle, didn't you?' commented Hugo.

'And a great help you were, I must say, staying in the car and having a cosy little nap. Why weren't you at my side, defending my sanity?'

'Would it have done any good if I had been?' he asked, surprising Lady Amanda into a thoughtful silence.

'I don't suppose it would have made the slightest difference,' she eventually admitted.

'Beauchamp told me to stay put, so that I wouldn't be associated with you. I know we were seen together at the funeral, but if I wasn't known to be with you on this ill-fated little expedition this evening, perhaps I may not automatically be assumed to be your "partner in crime",' Hugo explained.

'Cunning old Beauchamp!' she exclaimed. 'That means we can still use you as an agent, Hugo.'

'Not on your life!' he blurted out. 'Not after tonight. Now, tell me all about it; it must have been awful.' Not only did Hugo long for the details of the adventure he had slept through, but he knew, if he got Lady Amanda going, she would talk herself into a better mood, just by stealing the limelight, and telling a story in which she was the central character.

Back at Belchester Towers, Beauchamp efficiently produced mugs of cocoa, and the pair of elderly amateur sleuths made their way to bed, both eager for the oblivion that a good night's sleep would offer them.

Chapter Fourteen

No one in Belchester Towers rose early the next morning, and, as Lady Amanda Holmes and Dr Hugo Watson straggled downstairs, Beauchamp suggested that they lie low for a bit, and quit the sleuthing just for a while. He advised them that the bringing to justice of the evil Moriarty could be delayed, at least until they had their strength back, as Lestrade would never get the thing sorted out on his own. Maybe they could occupy themselves in some other, more innocent, way, as today was Sunday.

Lady Amanda gave the idea her best attention, then nodded her head in decision, and announced, 'I know what we'll do! We'll go over to Enid Tweedie's place and give it that airing I promised myself we'd do, before she returned home. You can come too, Beauchamp, for "the heavy". It wouldn't be right for a batty, fragile old biddy like myself to be taxed too much physically, now would it?'

'No, my lady,' answered Beauchamp, wooden-faced. Would he never be allowed to forget what had been said the previous evening? That the expediency and quick-wittedness that had extracted her from a very uncomfortable position the night before, and had been the only possible means of removing her from a situation that might have ended in her arrest, had not seemed to have occurred to her, yet.

As a sort of apology (although he didn't see what he had to apologise for) he made them a sumptuous breakfast that included such little treats as kidneys and kedgeree, and left them to help themselves. After all, he had saved some for himself, and his portion awaited him in the kitchen, keeping warm in the slowly cooling oven.

At ten o'clock, Lady Amanda presented herself in the kitchen, demanded to be allowed to raid the cupboard of cleaning products and equipment, and ordered him to load the vacuum cleaner into the boot of the Rolls.

When he returned from this errand, he found her in the middle of the kitchen, standing beside a broom, dustpan and brush, and mop and bucket, with a carrier bag clutched in each hand. 'I've gathered up polish, bleach, scouring powder, cloths, air freshener, lavatory cleaner, and that spray stuff that's supposed to eliminate foul odours. That should do us, shouldn't it?' she asked.

'You seem to have covered most things, my lady, but may I suggest a glass cleaner as well, for windows and mirrors?' Beauchamp replied.

'If you must! I'll get some out of your cupboard, and you can start loading this stuff into the boot, while I go and boot Hugo up the backside, to get *his* engine running. The exercise of a bit of cleaning will do his stiff old joints good – get some movement back into them,' she stated, and stumped out of the room, in search of the aforementioned unfortunate Hugo, who didn't know what was about to hit him, and by the time he spotted the whirlwind that was Lady Amanda, would not find himself in a suitable position to escape what was about to happen to him.

Poor Hugo was discovered behind an open copy of a Sunday newspaper, taking a casual look at the main news. Lady Amanda, rather in the manner of Beauchamp, approached him without a sound to alert him, and he suddenly found the newspaper torn from his grasp, and was then hauled unceremoniously to his feet.

'Look lively, Hugo!' she boomed, causing him to shrink away from this virago that had suddenly disturbed his Sunday morning musings. 'We're off to Enid's to get the place ready for her return home. Come on! Chop-chop! Haven't got time to waste!'

'I say, Manda, old bean. Give a chap a chance to digest his breakfast, won't you? The world won't come to an end if we don't go this very minute, will it?'

'It might! You never know. Now, look lively, and get yourself out of the house and into the Rolls. Operation Airing Enid is about to begin!'

It was, of course, useless to try to reason with Lady Amanda, when she was in one of her get-up-and-go moods, and so he trailed listlessly behind her, like a naughty schoolboy, approaching the room used for detention.

Enid Tweedie's tiny house was in a road un-edifyingly named 'Plague Alley', and this name seemed to have shaped her life. She had spent many years of her life in and out of hospital, having this altered or that removed, thus living up to the suffering implied in the name of the street where she lived.

The house fronted straight out on to the pavement, with no front garden dividing it from the narrow walkway. It had two bedrooms upstairs, and only a living room and a kitchen downstairs, a ramshackle bathroom having been tacked on to the back of it, somewhere back in the mists of time. Its number was thirteen, and this seemed appropriate, too, given Enid's unfortunate medical history.

She lived here with her aged mother, and an evil-smelling, and even fouler-tempered cat, the name of which, Lady Amanda had never bothered to enquire after, knowing only that Enid loved it dearly, as if it had been one of her own children.

Producing the key that Enid had previously bestowed on her from her handbag, Lady Amanda opened the door, and the three of them backed away, as a foul stench rushed out to engulf them in its greeting.

'What, in the name of all that's holy, is that ghastly smell?' asked Hugo, removing a handkerchief from his trouser pocket, and clasping it to his face. 'I could do with one of those old-fashioned vinaigrette things. We're surely not going in there, are we?'

'I'd forgotten about her mother's cigars,' said Lady Amanda, coughing in a ladylike way, behind her hand. 'The smell, as I understand it,' she went on, 'is comprised of the copious amounts of wee-wee with which Enid's mother generously sprinkles every piece of soft furnishing she comes into contact with.

'There is an additional layer added by that stinky old cat of hers, that not only smells of dead cat, but also pees everywhere, marking its territory, I suppose. The final ingredient is the lingering whiff of the small cigars which Enid's mother has recently taken to smoking. She had decided, apparently, that she wasn't getting the best value out of her old age pension, and took up the foul things to augment the gin she purchased, to make life a bit more bearable for the poor old thing that she considers herself to be.

'I haven't actually been here since she started smoking them, but I shall advise Enid to dissuade her from continuing to do so. The old dear's waited on hand, foot, and finger, and I don't see why she should be allowed to choke her daughter to death, just because she's got nothing better to spend her money on.

'I'll go in first, and open all the windows, and the back door, and then, when it's cleared a bit, you can bring all the gear in, and we can get started,' concluded Lady Amanda Golightly, carer for of old cleaners, and narrator of family histories.

A few minutes later, Beauchamp led the way, discharging a white cloud of air freshener before him, as he made his way into the pungent little dwelling. Hugo followed behind, reluctantly, his handkerchief still held to his nose. Fortunately for him, he still carried on the habit, learnt from his father, of sprinkling his handkerchiefs with cologne, and this scent, clasped to his face as it was, gave him the courage to follow Beauchamp.

Lady Amanda was already busy, throwing the cushions from the sofa and armchairs into the back yard, so that they could take the air. She had also gathered all the dishcloths, tea towels and bathroom towels she could lay her hands on, and the washing machine was already chugging away. With the windows open wide, the place already smelled better, and Beauchamp took charge of the vacuum cleaner, while Lady Amanda sat Hugo down at a small dining table with some brass ornaments, cleaner and a cloth.

'That shouldn't prove too strenuous for you, Hugo, old chum,' she trilled, always happy when she was bossing other people around. 'Get those gleaming, and it'll make all the difference to the end result.'

At one-thirty, they took a break, Beauchamp fetching boxes of sandwiches and flasks of coffee, which he had somehow found the time to prepare before they left, from the boot of the Rolls.

'I don't know how you do it, Beauchamp!' declared Lady Amanda. 'I thought we'd have to send out for fish and chips.'

'No chance of that, on a Sunday, if you don't mind me mentioning it, my lady,' he replied then added, very quietly under his breath, 'and it's Beecham!'

'Oh, smoked salmon and cucumber with horseradish,' declared Hugo, after his first bite. 'My absolute favourite, Beauchamp, you clever old stick. I hope Amanda knows what a treasure you are, and pays you accordingly.'

With as much dignity as he could muster, given that he was covered in dust, his normally immaculate clothing dirt-smeared and begrimed, Beauchamp replied, 'I am perfectly happy with the remuneration that Lady Amanda accords to be my due,' and bridled a little, at so coarse a mention of financial matters while eating.

By four-thirty, they had done as much as their energy would allow, the place was looking sparkling, and smelling much better, and Lady Amanda was having a last spray around with, first the air freshener, then with the fabric freshener.

'That should do!' she declared. 'Enid will be delighted when she gets back, but I'm going to advise her not to let her sister know that she's home. The longer she can keep that evil-smelling old witch of a mother of hers out of this place, the better. I'm going to suggest that she approach the local authority, with a view to getting her into a home. I'd love to see what they made of her at the Birdlings, and I might even get Enid to agree, now that she's stayed there, and found it very accommodating.'

'I say, what a topping idea, old thing,' agreed Hugo. 'If staying in that dreadful place is her idea of heaven, then she surely needs a lucky break in life, don't you agree?'

'I shall do my utmost to persuade her that her mother would be much better off, in the tender care of the place that has so admirably suited her, and I'm pretty certain she'll agree. What do you think, Beauchamp?'

'I,' intoned Beauchamp, 'am not paid to think, my lady.'

On arrival back at Belchester Towers, Beauchamp, usually the most stoic of characters, gave a yelp of alarm, as the car approached the frontage.

'Whatever is it, Beauchamp?' asked Lady Amanda, thoroughly shaken. It must be something dreadful, if Beauchamp had reacted in such an atypical way.

'The front doors are wide open, my lady,' he informed her, a quaver in his voice. 'It would appear that we have, or have had, intruders. Does my lady have her mobile telephone apparatus with her?' he asked, putting the Rolls into reverse, and moving it out of view from the front of the property, sensibly placing it behind a clump of large trees.

'Most certainly, Beauchamp. It's in my handbag.'

'Then may I suggest most respectfully, my lady, that the police are informed?' he advised her.

Of course, it was Inspector Moody who attended the call-out, and very scathing he was too, of the circumstances of his summoning.

'Are you sure the silly old biddy didn't just forget to close the doors, when you went out?' he asked Hugo, a malicious gleam in his eye.

'Lady Amanda is not a silly old biddy, and I personally saw Beauchamp both close and lock them, before he got into the Rolls,' Hugo answered, as insolently as he could manage given his innate good manners.

'Does anyone else have a key to the property?' Moody enquired, and was referred by Hugo to Beauchamp, who was waiting in stand-by mode, should he be able to provide any help.

'Lady Amanda has no relatives, and rarely entertains. To my knowledge, no one has keys to the property, except Lady Amanda and myself,' he replied with dignity.

'Has anything been taken – stolen,' the inspector continued.

'Nothing,' confirmed the fount of all wisdom that was Beauchamp, 'but several things have been moved from their usual places.'

'Such as?' Inspector Moody showed a reluctant interest in this piece of information.

'The ormolu clock that you may observe on the mantelpiece,' began Beauchamp, 'was originally on the mantelpiece in the dining room. And here, in the drawing room, the bronze you may observe on the low table was on the mantelpiece in here.

'Similarly, there are things which seem to have been taken from the library and put in the study, and things which have migrated from the study to the library,' he concluded.

'And you're perfectly sure that your employer,' here, Moody gave Lady Amanda a malevolent stare, 'did not move these things without your knowledge, before you left the house this morning?'

'Absolutely sure, Inspector. I was last to leave the property and, if you would take the care to notice the objects which have been moved, they are all too bulky and heavy for Lady Amanda to have moved on her own.'

'Could Mr Chumley-Wumley-Doodle have helped her?' Moody asked, with a sneer in his voice at the complexity and calibre of Hugo's triple-barrelled surname.

'Mr Cholmondley-Crichton-Crump has neither the strength nor the mobility to undertake such an exercise, Inspector,' Beauchamp informed the policeman, pronouncing Hugo's name with absolute precision, maintaining his dignity with difficulty, and fighting a powerful urge to give the inspector the benefit of a 'bunch of fives', Beauchamp-style. He had been a boxing champion in the army, and felt that he would soon show he hadn't lost his touch, if he let fly.

'I should request that you all refrain from touching the objects that have been moved, and I shall send a man along to dust them all for fingerprints. If anyone else has handled them, we'll soon find out who,' he informed them, in the most pompous of voices, and incorrect grammar.

'Not if the person who handled them wore gloves.' Lady Amanda had spoken for the first time since Inspector Moody had arrived, and her voice had a sharp, sarcastic edge to it. Moody chose to ignore her, and instead, warned Beauchamp and Hugo to keep a good eye on old

Wandering Winnie, or they'd have him to answer to.

When the door had closed behind him, the two men put their fingers in their ears, in anticipation of Lady Amanda's no doubt violent reaction, to being treated as if she were soft in the head, but were rewarded with an unexpected silence.

'This break-in is Foster's doing,' she declared, in perfectly reasonable tones. 'We've got him rattled, and he's trying to rattle us back. It's as clear as the nose on your face. He's left us a message which he didn't need to write down. "I know who you are and where you live, and I can get at you whenever I want to, so leave me alone, and I'll leave you alone". Don't you agree?' she asked, her head on one side like a bird's, as she awaited an answer.

Beauchamp slowly exhaled, suddenly aware that he had been holding his breath, while awaiting Lady Amanda's response to the policeman's visit, and now chose to hold his peace. Hugo, however, spoke up. 'Do you really think he'd do that sort of thing, Manda?' he asked.

'I expect he'd do that, and a lot more, if he could get away with three killings, scot free, and keep all the money he's inherited, as a result of his murderous misdeeds,' she answered. 'You take my word for it – he's out to scare us. Well, I don't scare that easily, and I'm not giving up.'

'Well, at least you can keep yourself out of mischief, tomorrow,' declared Hugo. 'We're taking Enid Tweedie back to her own home. A good deed like that, after all the work we've done today, ought to keep you on the straight and narrow for at least a day, and by then, maybe you'll have simmered down.

A few minutes after Lady Amanda went up to her room that night, there was a piercing scream and Beauchamp appeared at the foot of the stairs as if by magic, mounting them as if the house was afire. Hugo made straight for the lift, and set it in painfully slow motion, towards the source of the scream. The lift might be slow, but Hugo was considerably slower, and was aware of this fact. This was his quickest route to his old friend's aid.

When he finally exited the little box and entered Lady Amanda's room, he found her sitting on the stool at her dressing table, wringing her hands, and evidently distraught, Beauchamp standing by her side, waiting to see if there were anything he could fetch for her or do, to make her feel better.

The bedclothes were pulled back, and on the bottom sheet, lay a sheet of paper, with letters cut from newsprint stuck on to it. Hugo approached the bed, and leaned down to read what was spelled out on the sheet of paper, being careful not to touch it. He read: *You won't hear or see me approach, but I shall destroy you with a flick of my finger.*

Beauchamp made his exit before Hugo could react. When he did, it was with horror. 'Manda, this is a death threat! What are you going to do about it? He's killed before, and nobody suspects him of anything. You have to take this to the police.'

'What's the point, Hugo? Inspector Moody already thinks I'm in the throes of Alzheimer's, and won't listen to a word I say. He probably thinks you're in your dotage, too. And as for Beauchamp, he probably believes, and quite rightly so, in my opinion, that he would do anything within his power, to avoid trouble or scandal in The Family.'

Hugo heard the capital letters, and responded, 'You're quite sure of that, are you?'

'Definitely! Beauchamp will be loyal to the end, whether that be my end, or his.'

The speaking of his name appeared to conjure Beauchamp up out of the ether, and he returned to the room with a plastic bag and a pair of silver sugar-nips in his hands. 'I'll just deal with this, my lady, then you can get into bed, and get some rest, after all the physical work

156

you have undertaken today. You must be very tired.'

'Thank you, Beauchamp. It's most thoughtful of you to think of preserving the evidence,' Lady Amanda praised him.

Very quietly; even softer than a whisper, came the words, 'That's *Beecham*!'

Chapter Fifteen

The following morning dawned bright and sunny, but with a stiffening breeze that promised less fair weather later in the day. Beauchamp was up and at his duties at his normal hour, but once again Lady Amanda and Hugo were late to rise.

Lady Amanda had had difficulty sleeping, and so had turned to one of her favourite Conan Doyle books, reading into the small hours, before she finally turned out her light. Hugo had sought no such consolation and calm in books, for that was not his way, and tossed and turned, suffering from nightmares, when he finally dropped off to sleep, about five o'clock.

Both of them looked tired and drawn, when they met for breakfast, and neither of them had much appetite. So concerned was Beauchamp, that he was moved to speech. 'You need to eat. You've got a busy day ahead of you, moving Mrs Tweedie out of the nursing home and back into her own house, and no doubt she'll need some shopping done. How are you going to achieve that, if you don't have a bite inside yourselves?' he asked, with concern.

Lady Amanda was so surprised by this unprecedented show of interest in her well-being, that she was moved to speech. 'Thank you for your concern, Beauchamp. What you say is good advice, and I think we both had better act on it. Come on, Hugo! That's a lovely kipper you've got in front of you. Don't let it go to waste. How are you ever going to get the machine to work, if you have no fuel in the engine? That reminds me, you haven't had the

159

opportunity to have a proper ride on that motorised tricycle, yet, have you? We'll have to get that organised *tout de suite.'*

Hugo, suddenly becoming aware that his personal safety was to be put at risk again, responded with, 'No fear, Manda! You'll not get me on that devil's contraption while I'm feeling like this.'

'Then get that kipper down your neck, and have some toast and marmalade. Beauchamp's put your favourite thick-cut lemon out for you. We've got a job of work to do today and I need you on tip-top form.'

Enid needed to vacate her room at The Birdlings by noon, and thus they set off about eleven o'clock, with a picnic lunch in the boot of the Rolls, so that they should not have to go shopping, until after they'd broken bread with her.

Hugo had eventually given in and eaten a fairly substantial breakfast, feeling much better for his effort. He was quite looking forward to seeing Enid's face, when she saw her clean and tidy (not to mention fresh-smelling) home on her return.

Both of them were silent on the drive into Belchester, each of them lost in thought, going over what had happened, not only in the last couple of days, but in the ten days since Lady Amanda had appeared so unexpectedly and abruptly in Hugo's life, and whisked him off to a completely different existence.

Hugo was not sure what he thought about this rapid change in his circumstances. While he was extremely grateful to be released from his former misery in the home, he was not sure how he felt about the added excitement that Lady Amanda had introduced into his formerly dull existence. He thought he quite liked it, but finally decided not to make up his mind, until time had proved that neither of them were about to be set upon by Mr Derek Foster.

Lady Amanda was having similar thoughts. She was

getting used to having Hugo around, but it made a huge difference to her normal behaviour. The excitement, she definitely liked. She assumed that time would provide familiarity with Hugo's constant presence. Whatever happened, at least he had livened her up a bit. What a bit of luck it had been, there being a murder, just when the two of them were reunited, after so many years. Well, not so lucky for poor old Reggie, but it had certainly provided something for them to get their teeth into.

Beauchamp, although one may not have thought so, also had his own opinion on the past ten days. He hadn't seen Lady Amanda so animated for a long time, and she certainly seemed brighter since Mr Cholmondley-Crichton-Crump had come to stay. Whether this was because of the murder, or because of Hugo's company, he could not be sure, but he hoped that she would continue to be so animated, and not come to any harm from this situation in which she had involved them all.

Enid Tweedie had her suitcase packed and was sitting on the bed in the room she had occupied for the last week, waiting for them. She looked healthy and happy; hardly recognisable as the Enid Lady Amanda had known for so long.

'Oh, Lady Amanda!' she exclaimed as Lady A and Hugo entered the room. 'I've had such a lovely time here, and made so many new friends. I can't thank you enough for your generosity. I feel like a new woman!'

'You look like one, too. I've never seen your cheeks so rosy, and I do believe you've put on a little bit of weight,' observed Lady Amanda.

'And it's all thanks to you!' the soon-to- be ex-inmate enthused. 'I shall have so much more energy when I get home. I shall be round that house like an electric eel.'

As Hugo gallantly hefted her suitcase, there was a discreet knock at the door, and Nurse Plunkett entered, with another couple of members of staff. 'We're really going to miss you, Enid,' Nurse Plunkett declared, with tears forming in her eyes. 'You've been the life and soul of this place, with all those hilarious tales about your family. We're going to miss you terribly.'

This sentiment was echoed by the other two who had accompanied her, and even Matron made an appearance at the door, to pay her fond farewells. 'Such a surprise to find out what a charming friend you have in Enid,' she declared, still at daggers drawn with Lady Amanda, but delighted with her now-departing patient.

'Do come in to visit us sometime, won't you?' pleaded one of the other nurses, and received a beaming smile from Enid, in return.

'Of course I will, my dear. It will be my pleasure!'

'Come along, Enid!' exhorted Lady Amanda, thoroughly fed-up with all this sloppy sentiment, with Enid Tweedie, of all people, at its centre. She'd always found the woman dull beyond belief, and found it hard to believe her to be a fount of humorous stories and anecdotes. Lady Amanda didn't realise it, but sometimes she was jealous of other people's popularity.

The six people from the room made a gay parade as they passed down the corridor towards the exit, and Lady Amanda wouldn't have been surprised if someone had produced a tambourine, and encouraged them all to skip along and dance. Who would have thought that drab little Enid Tweedie could be cast as a 'Pied Piper' character?

The Rolls drew up in front of Enid's tiny house, nearly as long as the house was broad, its very presence turning the house into the image of a veritable playhouse for children.

As Beauchamp collected her luggage from the boot, Lady Amanda and Hugo accompanied her to the front door, waiting for her to unlock it and see the wonders they had wrought within, especially for her homecoming.

Stepping inside, straight into the living room, there being no space to accommodate an entrance hall, Enid looked around her with tears in her eyes, and said, 'Home, sweet home. There's nowhere like it. And just as I left it when I went into hospital.'

'Not quite!' boomed Lady Amanda's voice. 'We three spent all day yesterday giving it a good "bottoming". Can't you see the difference? Can you not *smell* the difference?'

Enid stood for a moment in thought. 'Yes,' she agreed. 'I can see you've been round with a duster. That was very kind of you, but there's a terrible aroma of cheap scent in here. I wonder where it's come from.'

Lady Amanda rolled her eyes, but stilled her mouth, as both Beauchamp and Hugo gave her the most ferocious glares. Some saints, she thought, would go ever unrewarded, their works unrecognised by those who couldn't see beyond the ends of their noses.

'We've brought a picnic lunch,' she informed Enid, 'then we can make a shopping list and get you in some supplies. What about your mother?'

'Mother's staying where she is!' Enid declared. They've got a big colour telly there, and my sister says her cigar smoke keeps her husband out from under her feet. She says she hasn't had such a peaceful life since before she got married. That only leaves my Oscar to be accounted for.'

'That mangy old cat of yours?' enquired Lady Amanda, wrinkling her nose in disgust.

Here, Beauchamp spoke up. 'Before I brought in the luggage, a lady from the house next door attracted my attention, and informed me that the cat had taken up residence with her, since its owner was away in hospital so much,' he informed them.

'Well, with that smelly old witch of a mother of yours decamped, and that stinking old cat of yours peeing on someone else's furniture for a change, life should take a turn for the better for you, Enid,' Lady Amanda offered, judge and jury on the new circumstances in which Enid found herself.

'But what shall I do all day, without Mother and Oscar?' she wailed.

'Get yourself a life, woman!' Lady Amanda advised her. 'You'll have time for all those things you said you always wanted to do – join the WI, do a cookery course, learn to embroider ... There are heaps of things you've mentioned to me, in the past, that you simply didn't have time for, and longed to do.'

'I did, didn't I?' replied Enid. 'And you're right! I shall start right away.'

'Just don't forget you're due up at The Towers on Friday for the 'heavy', as always.'

'Of course I won't. I love working in such a wonderful old home, and I shall be there on the dot of nine. But it won't be the same.'

'Won't be the same as what?' asked Lady Amanda, not quite catching Enid's line of thought.

'I shan't be an undercover agent any more. I found that very exciting.'

'Well, you never know. You might get to do it again, sometime in the future.'

'I do hope so. You lead such an exciting life.'

'And so shall you now, Enid, my dear,' Lady Amanda assured her, 'now you've got a bit of freedom back.'

'Yes, I expect I shall. Thank you all, for what you've done for me.'

That evening, after a good slug of Strangeways to Oldham, Lady Amanda returned to the subject that had been waiting to infect her mind since the day before. 'I need to get *into* that chap Foster's home,' she declared, apropos of nothing.

'You can't be serious, Manda! Have you forgotten already, that beastly note he left in your bed last night?'

asked Hugo, aghast at her bold intention. 'He's already threatened your life, and now you plan to go right into the lion's den?' He could hardly believe his ears.

At that moment the telephone rang, and they could hear Beauchamp answer it in the hall. The instrument seemed to be giving him some trouble, as they could hear him say, 'Hello. Hello. Is there anybody there?' a bit like a quack medium at the end of the pier in a seaside resort.

There was a discreet clatter, as he replaced the receiver of the old-fashioned telephone back in its cradle, and he entered the room to inform them, 'Must have been a wrong number, my lady. There was no one on the other end of the line.'

The phone rang again, and Beauchamp left the room with unhurried steps, to answer it again.

The result was the same as before, and Beauchamp gave it as his solemn opinion that there was something wrong with the line. After all, the wind was getting up, and it seemed that they were in for some stormy weather, in the very near future.

'You're no doubt correct, Beauchamp. A line down, or something. Nothing to bother us, though. If anyone really wants to get in touch, they'll leave it until they can get through properly,' decided Lady Amanda, returning to her abandoned conversation with Hugo.

'There must be some evidence in that house that I could give to Inspector Moody, to make him take me seriously,' she declared, spearing Hugo with a gaze that dared him to disagree.

'What do you expect to find, Manda? A recipe book with Strangeways to Oldham marked, and 'poison' added to the list of ingredients? He's not that stupid. He's been clever enough, so far. Why should he give himself away with something stupid like that?

'He's got your number, Manda, and he's let you know that he knows that you know – blast! That sounded like a riddle, but you know what I mean. You need to face the fact that the man's dangerous, and wouldn't hesitate to make you his next victim.'

'Tosh! He's an amateur!'

'I beg to differ. It's you who are the amateur. He's killed three people. I consider, personally, that that gives him professional status; especially as no one but we two suspect him of any wrongdoing whatsoever.'

The telephone rang again, a further interruption to this, now heated, discussion and, knowing that Beauchamp was in the kitchen preparing dinner, Lady Amanda rose to answer it. Lifting the receiver to her ear, she intoned the number and waited for a reply, but there was nothing but silence on the line. No, hang on a minute! She could just discern the soft susurration of breathing.

'Hello. Hello. Who is this?' she asked, her voice rising with impatience.

'Gonna get you!' The words were barely louder than a breath, but she was sure she heard them, before the connection was broken by whoever was at the other end of the line.

Dropping the handset in her surprise, she called for Hugo, and stood stock still with shock, waiting for her mind to tell her she had imagined it, but it stubbornly refused to try to persuade her that this was the case.

'Whatever's the matter?' asked Hugo solicitously, as he tottered out of the drawing room.

'There was someone on the phone,' she announced starkly.

'There usually is, when it rings,' offered Hugo, with maddening logic.

'I think it was *him*!' She spoke quietly, as if she suspected that they were being eavesdropped on by some unidentified presence.

'Him who?' asked Hugo, ungrammatically.

'Him! Foster!' Lady Amanda replied, in an urgent

whisper.

'What did he say?' Hugo continued with his maddeningly calm enquiries.

'He just said, "Gonna get you," but it was barely a whisper. I could hear him breathing down the phone, then he said *that*, and it was so quiet, that for a moment, I thought I'd imagined it. But I didn't Hugo, I really didn't!'

'There, there, old girl,' Hugo soothed, putting his arm around her shoulder in an uncharacteristically affectionate manner. 'We'll let Beauchamp know, at dinner, what's happened, and he can make sure that the house is locked up as tight as a drum tonight – keep us all safe till the morning. Everything always looks better in daylight, don't you think?'

Beauchamp locked every door and window, as soon as he was informed of the incident that had so unsettled Lady Amanda, and suggested that they contact the police in the morning. 'After all, my lady, even if he doesn't intend to carry events any further, he is, at the very least, conducting a campaign of terror against you, and he needs to be stopped, before things get out of hand.'

'Was the house locked up yesterday, Beauchamp?' asked Lady Amanda, timidly.

'It was, indeed, my lady,' Beauchamp assured her.

'Then how the dickens did he get in to leave a note under my bedclothes?' she asked, less timidly, and in a more accusatory tone.

'I have no idea, my lady, but I shall do my utmost to ensure that there is no way into Belchester Towers this night.'

Like a 'B' movie horror, there was a flicker of lightning, and an almighty crash of thunder, and the rain started to pelt down with a real vengeance.

'Oh, good grief!' shrieked Lady Amanda, Hugo was seen visibly to jump in his chair, and even Beauchamp raised an eyebrow in surprise.

'Beauchamp, would you be so kind as to make up a bed for me in the room next to Hugo's? I'm feeling rather nervous tonight, and don't consider that my bedroom is a good place to spend the night. After all, he knows where I usually sleep. He evidently had no trouble finding my room to place that note, and I don't want to spend tonight in the same room – just in case,' she ended rather lamely.

'No sooner said, than done, my lady,' confirmed Beauchamp, and left the room, forgetting, in his genuine concern for her safety, to whisper 'Beecham'.

Chapter Sixteen

The storm worsened, and the wind howled in the multitude of chimneys in the old house, and bent the trees in the grounds, in its strength. It soughed in the eaves, and blew hitherto undisturbed detritus into new life, sending it wheeling and spinning across the lawns like the phantoms of discarded lives.

Thunder rolled round the sky, a tympanic accompaniment to the lightning, providing one of nature's most spectacular examples of *son et lumière*, out-performing anything that man, in his humble place in the great scheme of planetary life, could imitate.

Rain bounced from the ground, to make a second impact a fraction of a second later, and plants were battered by its bullet-like impacts. This was no night to be out and about, for either human or animal. The weather waged a war with the area, its power unchallengeable, its dominance supreme.

Beauchamp systematically did his rounds of all the means of ingress, carefully locking that which was unfastened, and checking that which was already locked. The care with which he disposed of this duty was witness to the anxiety that he was suffering. A man not easily ruffled, his feathers were well and truly fluffed up tonight.

Unfazed by many an event that would have left lesser mortals trembling, he found himself to be strangely unsettled by the silent telephone calls, and even more alarmed by that received by Lady Amanda, when examined together with the note, that had mysteriously appeared in his employer's bed, the previous night.

This task completed to his satisfaction, he adjourned to the kitchen to make a cup of cocoa for them all. Cocoa was the ultimate comfort, at bedtime, especially when one was feeling a little ill at ease. As he approached the drawing room with his tray, the telephone rang again, and Lady Amanda appeared in the hall, to answer its urgent summons.

He halted to listen to what would happen, and observed her listening in silence, a look of undiluted horror spreading across her face. Then she repeated 'hello' thrice over, before taking the receiver from her ear and staring at it suspiciously, and reaching down to press repeatedly on the connection bar, in the manner of someone in the past, trying to attract the attention of the old-fashioned operator service, which used to be the only way to get a call put through.

'Is everything all right, my lady?' he asked, putting down the tray on a half-moon hall table.

Without a word, she held out the receiver in offering, and he took it from her and put it to his own ear. Silence! That's all there was. No dial tone. No furtive breathing. Either the storm had brought down the lines, or they had had their telephone line deliberately cut.

'Did he say anything, my lady?' enquired Beauchamp.

'He – he – he said he could see my house,' she told him, her voice breaking up with fear.

'He s-said he could see m-my h-house, and soon he'd b-be able to s-see *me*,' she informed her intrepid manservant.

Not wishing to alarm Lady Amanda any further, he handed back the receiver, and reassured her that it was probably just a crank, or a crossed line, and the breakage that occurred was, no doubt, due to damage caused by the storm, which was still raging round the countryside. 'Come on back to the dining room, and forget all about it, my lady,' he encouraged her. 'I have a tray of cocoa here, to relax you before you go to bed.'

But Beauchamp was worried. Damned worried!

As Lady Amanda and Hugo repaired to their separate rooms, she asked Hugo if he would mind if she left the adjoining door open for the night. She explained that it would make her feel safer, to know that he would hear her if anything befell her, and she, him. Hugo raised no objection, feeling that, if he should need assistance in the night, it would be easier to rouse her without a sixty-pound lump of oak muffling his voice, and creating a physical barrier between them.

Both of them lay in their separate beds, listening to the ravages of the storm, neither of them in the least inclined to go to sleep, each taunted by worries about their own safety, and that of the other. Beauchamp was an admirable chap, but he couldn't be everywhere at once, and the chances of him being anywhere in the vicinity of their adjoining rooms, should anything untoward occur, were slight indeed.

So, neither of them actively sought sleep, but it hunted them down, and gradually overcame their worries and fears, as it does most nights of one's life. By one o'clock, they were both sleeping peacefully, the only sounds in that part of the house, apart from the storm, being the creaking of old wood, and the steady 'tick-tock' of the long-case clock in the hall, the sound of which had always been particularly penetrating.

At about three o'clock, Lady Amanda suddenly awoke, every nerve in her body tingling, with the absolute certainty that she had been awoken by an alien sound, somewhere within the house. Sitting up cautiously, she strained her ears to listen, and there it was again. There was someone in the cellars. She knew Beauchamp wouldn't be so insensitive as to do something like that,

171

considering the state their nerves were in. They had an intruder. Again!

As quietly as she could, she got out of bed, and crept into Hugo's room. He was lying on his back, snoring gently, as a gentleman should. Approaching his inert body, she shook him gently by the shoulder to wake him.

She shook him again, rather more vigorously this time, and still he did not stir. In one final effort, she put one hand over his mouth, and pinched his nostrils together with her other hand. That always worked, and it proved so in this case, as she had known it would. The feeling of being suffocated was a great aid in waking oneself up.

'Whaaa …!' gasped Hugo, struggling for breath, and gazing wild-eyed about him, to discover the cause of his discomfort. He had left the curtains undrawn, and was able, instantly, to recognise Lady Amanda's figure, standing at the bedside.

'What's up?' he asked abruptly, cross about having his repose disturbed.

'Shh!' she admonished him. 'I can hear someone in the cellars. We've got to hide.'

'Are you mad, Manda?' he hissed.

'Certainly not! But I am sure that what I've heard, twice now, was someone skulking about in the cellars. We've got to get out of here.'

'Where do you suggest we go?' Hugo was still not quite with it.

'Up, Hugo. Up! I'm not sure whether Beauchamp's on patrol, or fast asleep. All I know is that we've got to find somewhere to hide, before he finds us and does us harm. Come on, get out of bed and follow me.' Unused to having such a new-fangled gadget as a telephone, she often forgot its existence.

With great reluctance, Hugo rose from his bed and put on his slippers but, as he reached for his dressing gown, Lady Amanda's voice hissed, 'We haven't got time for

172

that, nor for hats, scarves, comforters or gloves. Come on, Hugo. We've got to get out of here now!' and clutching only her handbag, she dragged him out into the hall, and headed for the staircase.

'I can't get upstairs that way,' Hugo whispered urgently. 'I'm not steady enough on my pins.'

'The lift then!' she decided.

'He'll hear us.'

'Yes, but if he's in the cellars, it'll take him some time to get to the hall, and we'll have hidden ourselves by then and, with any luck, the sound of the lift will have woken Beauchamp, and he'll be able to rush to our aid.'

A tremendous crash of thunder, like the crack of doom, broke above the estate, virtually simultaneously with its accompanying vivid flash of lightning, and the two of them scampered for the lift, as quickly as age and infirmity would allow.

As they waddled towards it, full steam ahead, Hugo hissed, 'If Beauchamp can hear us, so can he. He'll guess where we've gone, and come after us.'

'There are acres of space up there. Two more floors, and then the attics,' she hissed back, dragging him into the tiny cage of the lift, and closing the doors as quietly as she could. 'This thing only goes up to the first floor, as you know, but it'll give us a head start. I'll leave the cage doors open at the top, then he can't follow us. He'll probably go straight to my bedroom first, as he knows where it is.'

'If he follows us on foot, he'll be much quicker than if he uses this thing,' opined Hugo mournfully.

'Don't be so negative. If we're up against the wall, we fight, Hugo – like animals, if necessary. Now shut up, and save your breath for escape!'

The ascension of the lift was grindingly, painfully, slow, as well as noisy, exaggerating their anxiety and fear, rather than calming them with the fact that they were already in flight, and hadn't been caught, literally, napping. Sounds, as of someone making a bit of a din in the cellars, made their way up the shaft of the lift, further unsettling them.

At the top, Hugo, in his haste, accidentally pressed the 'down' button again, and it was only the quick-witted action of Lady Amanda, that stopped them arriving back at the point where their flight had started.

Exiting the unsettling little metal cage on the first floor, Lady Amanda espied Hugo's Zimmer frame, and hissed a question at him. 'What's that thing doing up here?' she asked.

'I brought it up in case I fancied a bit of exploration, ferreting around, that sort of thing. I could get to the lift downstairs, but thought I might wear myself out a bit up here, and would need it before I came down again.'

'Just shut up and grab it, NOW, then follow me down this corridor. We've got to be quick. He's much faster than us, and we've lost some of our head start because of that silly stunt of yours, with the lift.'

'It wasn't a stunt! It was a simple mistake. Sometimes you can be very judgemental, Manda,' hissed Hugo.

'Save your breath for fleeing, old stick. Come on, just a little faster.'

Hugo propelled his walker as fast as he could, but could not keep up the speed that Lady Amanda set. Eventually, she went back to where he was, opened a door, and pushed him inside a cupboard, casting his walking frame aside, and pressing her handbag on him, as she did so.

'I'm afraid it's the linen press for you, Hugo old boy,' she informed him, as she manhandled him inside the cupboard. 'They took the shelves out years ago, so there's loads of room. You shouldn't be too squashed. Just stay there nice and quietly until either Beauchamp or I come to fetch you out again. I can get on faster on my own.'

With that, she slammed the door on the highly confused

Hugo, and made her way as fast as she could manage, up the staircase to the second floor, this one a little less grand than that from the ground floor to the first.

From there, she supposed she would have to head for the attics, but, for now, she just had ambitions of reaching the next floor. One step at a time was how to achieve anything important. Try to tackle too many things at once and you scuppered your own efforts, and played right into your enemies' hands. She'd learnt that at school. During lacrosse practice!

Meanwhile, Hugo had found himself an old packing case to sit on, located by touch alone, and had settled himself to explore Lady A's handbag. He knew she normally carried a little torch in there, and thought that it might be comforting, just to have a little light in his hidey-hole.

Having located the torch, he used its small light (for its head was only half an inch in diameter) to locate a bag of mint imperials, and popped one into his mouth, to keep body and soul together, until someone turned up to tell him that the hue and cry was over, and it was safe for him to come out, and go back to bed again.

He decided to leave further investigations of the gargantuan handbag for his later entertainment, and sat, torch switched off, sucking his peppermint, perfectly content with life, provided it didn't involve him getting caught up in any actual fisticuffs.

From downstairs, there came a crash, and the sound of muffled swearing. Hugo immediately had a mental picture of the wheelchair that had been delivered for him, and the fact that he had left it just outside the door to the cellar steps. Whoever the intruder was, he must have come up from the cellar and run into it, not expecting something like that to be right across a doorway.

An enormous brattle of thunder sounded, the sliver of light at the foot of the cupboard door flickered, then was extinguished. The storm must have knocked out the electricity supply. That was in Manda's favour, he decided, as she had lived here all her life, and knew this house like the back of her hand.

A noise outside his hideaway implied that Foster, if that is who it was, was tackling the stairs to the first floor with some speed, and heading towards the cupboard. Hugo steeled himself for discovery, but instead, heard a howl of rage, as their pursuer had presumably got himself entangled with Hugo's walking frame now. He must not have noticed it, in the sudden lack of electrical lighting.

A similar crash became audible from the second floor, and the sound of someone swearing loudly and robustly. Golly, he thought, Manda must be terrified out of her mind, if she's cussing like that.

Whoever was outside the door of Hugo's temporary housing must have heard it too, for there were sounds of someone picking themselves up, and stamping towards the staircase to the second floor. He was on his way to get her, and there was no way Hugo could warn her of his approach.

Sunk in misery, he opened the handbag once again, more as something to occupy his mind, as sitting doing nothing would drive him to despair. What was that, down in the corner? Hugo scrabbled down to the bottom of the handbag, on a voyage of discovery.

Upstairs, on the second floor, Lady Amanda had got herself into a tangle with a clothes rail filled with old wire coat-hangers, the sudden loss of light having caused her to make this unfortunate collision. As she wrestled with the wretched things now, she could hear someone charging up the stairs towards the ballroom, where she was currently trying to untangle herself.

As she finally pulled herself free, there was a vivid explosion of light from outside, clearly showing her, standing at the far side of the vast space, and illuminating a crouched figure at the other end, apparently getting his bearings.

Without a moment's hesitation, she was off again, heading for a small, semi-concealed door behind which was the tiny, narrow staircase to the attics. Grabbing a chair that stood forlornly by itself, just this side of the door, she manhandled it through the small opening with her, and jammed it against the wooden door, which opened inwards on to the stairs. That should hold him for long enough for her to get herself hidden.

The attics of Belchester Towers had not been cleared since the house had been built, and consisted of a vast network of inter-connected spaces, housing all manner of discarded furniture, clothing, and general junk. Packing cases were strewn everywhere, a trap for the unwary, and old garments, once special, were suspended on hangers from beams, to wrap themselves round the heads of those who did not observe where they were going.

Lady Amanda knew exactly where she was going, and ducked and wove her way through the maze of detritus like an expert. Little had been added since she used to play up here as a child, and she knew her way through the labyrinth from long experience.

She and her friends used to play hide-and-seek in these attics when she was a youngster, and she knew some of the best places to conceal herself, where even her parents would not have discovered her should they have searched.

As she took herself to a cramped space in the middle of a collection of old tea-chests, she pulled down a curtain that hung from a beam, and draped it over her entire body. On one side of her was a suit of armour that would make a marvellous weapon, should her pursuer find her.

The wind up here was considerable, blowing in through the eaves as it did, and she almost didn't hear the sound of sirens wailing their way up the drive. Suddenly there was hope again, and she remembered, with triumph, that she had left her mobile phone in her handbag. Either Hugo had found it, and summoned help, or Beauchamp had become aware of the intruder, and alerted the authorities. Whichever it was, it didn't matter now, for help was on its way.

Suddenly she felt her bowels clench with fear again. Help might be arriving, but would it be in time to save her? Foster was out to get her, and she couldn't see him mildly surrendering himself, just because the police were outside. After all, he still had time to complete his mission, and goodness knows what story he'd come up with, but it would no doubt be a plausible one.

There was a kicking and scraping noise from the bottom of the little staircase, and she knew he was at the foot of the stairs, and hadn't passed by the door without noticing it, and realising its significance.

She heard the sound of wood giving way. That would be the old chair. It would never have made a successful barrier, but it must have been older than she thought. She had considered that it would last a little longer than it evidently had.

There they were now, footsteps on the staircase, leading right to her place of concealment. The steps, however, were slow, and she imagined him savouring his moment of victory, approaching it at a pace that would allow him maximum enjoyment, at her discovery.

Her heart raced, and she felt her mouth and throat go dry. Should she have wished to scream, she didn't believe she had the ability. Suddenly he spoke into the surrounding darkness.

'I know you're up here,' he murmured, and there was an evil little snickering noise. 'I know where you are,' his voice taunted her. 'And I'm coming to *get you*,' she heard.

Maybe, in his intensity of purpose, he hadn't heard the sirens, which heralded the arrival of the police. 'I've got a flask here, of your favourite cocktail,' he teased again, 'and I'm going to get you to drink it all up, like a good little girl.' His voice was getting closer and closer to her place of concealment.

In a fit of almost fatal folly, she found herself wanting to ask him which cocktail he had considered as her favourite, and had to bite hard on her bottom lip, to stop the words escaping from her mouth. She held her breath, and tried to keep every muscle absolutely still.

'I'm coming to get you, and I'm getting *warmer and warmer*,' the voice crooned on, and it did, indeed seem to be much closer to hand than it had been before. With a glance of absolute horror, she stared down, and saw his feet, just the other side of the suit of armour. What to do? What to do? She had to do something, or she'd be dead!.

Without giving it a conscious thought, she pushed with all her strength against the rusting metal structure and, using her feet as the main force, managed to unseat it and send it falling away from her. As it landed, she heard a scream close at hand and, suddenly, the lights went back on. She knew this, because light flooded up from the ballroom, along with the sound of running feet.

Inspector Moody tugged at the old-fashioned chain-pull that illuminated this part of the attics, and surveyed what lay before him. A man he recognised as Derek Foster lay on the floor, trying to struggle from beneath the weight of an elderly suit of armour. Lady Amanda Golightly was getting shakily to her feet, with a mouldering curtain over her, like a Regency-striped shroud.

Taking this scene in at a glance, he approached her and said, 'Lady Amanda Golightly, I arrest you for the actual bodily harm of Mr Derek Foster of,' here he stopped and searched his memory, 'number eleven Mogs End,' he concluded, smugly.

This rescue wasn't going at all the way Lady Amanda

had planned it.

Circumstances eventually sorted themselves out, Hugo was recovered from the old linen press, whence he had summoned help on the mobile phone he had discovered in Lady Amanda's handbag, and Beauchamp was discovered tied to a chair in his sitting room, a gag in his mouth, and a nasty lump on the head where Foster had used a cosh on him.

Although Moody had difficulty in accepting that Foster was the sinning party, and Lady Amanda the party sinned against, he had no choice but to believe her, when both Hugo and Beauchamp backed up her story.

'I say, Hugo, old chap, guess what I saw in the attics when I was up there?'

'No idea, Manda, but don't leave me in suspenders,' Hugo replied.

'The old Carstairs invalid chair with the cane-work back and seat. It was for Papa's mama. Apparently a few hand-picked officers were allowed to convalesce here, during the First World War, and these were what they used to get around in when they weren't quite the ticket. One of them was requisitioned for family use and, I'm afraid to say, was never handed in, and it's still up there. I thought we might be able to use that now, and send that new-fangled affair back to social services.'

'I shouldn't do anything rash, my lady. Should the seat prove to be perished with age, Mr Hugo might go straight through it, and we should probably come across him, effectively hog-tied, as it were,' Beauchamp felt compelled to suggest.

'Good idea, Beauchamp. I shouldn't like to have you come across me hog-tied by an invalid carriage, either,' concluded Hugo, with feeling.

Before he left, there was one thing Inspector Moody wanted to get to the bottom of. 'Would you care to explain to me why Mr Foster has so many bruises about his person?' he asked, wondering how Lady Amanda was going to talk her way out of that one.

'I'm afraid that's all my doing, Inspector. Terribly sorry,' Hugo apologised shame-facedly.

'Your doing?' Moody almost shouted. There was no way he could see this mild-mannered elderly gentleman inflicting violence on anything other than a wayward pillow in his bed.

'I fear that Mr Foster may have tripped over the modern wheelchair that Lady Amanda just mentioned. I'm afraid I stupidly left it just outside the cellar door. And then, when the lights went out, I believe he became entangled with my walking frame on the first floor landing.'

'He must have come through the wooden doors to the old coal chute. The padlock on those was always dodgy,' Lady Amanda added.

As Foster was led off in handcuffs, Moody turned to his erstwhile thorn-in-the-side, and said, 'I suppose you realise that this means two exhumations? He had his uncle cremated.'

'If justice is to be done, Inspector, they are inevitable. Should you need any more evidence, I have the original cocktail glass out of which Mr Reginald Pagnell took his last drink on this earth. It is currently locked in my safe for security reasons, and if you analyse what it once contained, I think that your laboratory will discover, not only poison, but the traces of a cocktail called Strangeways to Oldham,' she informed him, didactically.

'If you had only listened to me in the first place, maybe two of these three unfortunate deaths could have been avoided.' She was at her most imperious, as she addressed him, and he was suitably chastened by what he had discovered.

That did not, however, make him feel any more kindly

disposed towards her, and at her pretty little victory speech, he merely made a sour grimace, and left the premises, promising that she would be required to give evidence, should her speculation about how the three men had died prove to be correct.

He had also had PC Glenister in tow, and as he left, in pursuit of his superior, he looked at Lady Amanda and gave her a huge wink. 'I enjoyed that!' he murmured, as he went out through the door, then looked back over his shoulder and mouthed, 'Nice one, Lady Amanda!'

It was Wednesday evening, and all three of the occupants of Belchester Towers were sufficiently recovered and rested from their ordeal, to consider re-instating cocktail hour, which had been in abeyance for the last couple of days.

'I think we shall have champagne cocktails tonight, Beauchamp,' ordered Lady Amanda, sounding just like an elderly duchess bossing her staff around, so puffed up was she, at her own cleverness, and her triumph over the ill-mannered Inspector Moody. 'And do have one yourself,' she added magnanimously, as Beauchamp turned to leave the room.

Almost inaudibly, he muttered, 'I always do, my lady. And the name's still Beecham.'

'Well, Hugo,' she said, 'How are you enjoying living here?'

'It can be quite exciting,' replied Hugo diplomatically.

'Is everything to your satisfaction?' she asked, rather overdoing the Lady Bountiful impression.

'Except for the unusual experience of being pursued by a murderer,' he said, nodding his head for emphasis.

'That is not,' she retorted, 'part of the normal routine at The Towers. No, I meant everything else – food, laundry, your room, and so on.'

'Oh, that's all marvellous, and I do seem to be a lot

more sprightly than I was, when I arrived here.'

'You must be, Hugo,' Lady Amanda purred, 'if you've been leaving your invalid walker upstairs, and I don't believe we've used that wheelchair since you had that appointment with that rather strange Dr Updyke.'

'No, we haven't,' Hugo concurred.

'Champagne cocktails, my lady, Mr Hugo,' announced Beauchamp, entering the room with his usual silent tread, and making Lady Amanda, whose chair wasn't facing the door, start with surprise.

'Don't do that, Beauchamp. I've told you before. If you must move silently, please cough, or do something else to announce that you are about to appear in our midst without the slightest of warnings.'

'Yes, my lady.'

Lady Amanda and Hugo accepted their drinks, noticing that there was one left on the tray. Lady Amanda lifted her glass and toasted them with, 'Chin-chin,' (but in the French way – 'shin-shin'), which left Hugo staring uncomprehendingly at his lower legs. 'Glad to see you took me at my word, and mixed one for yourself,' she said, but fell silent when there was a ring at the doorbell.

'Who can that be, at this time of night?' asked Lady Amanda, not expecting any answer.

'How can we possibly know that before we open the door?' replied Hugo, his usual common sense making itself known.

'No, I mean, we're having our little drinkies late, tonight. It's nearly ten o'clock. No one should be making house calls at this time of night.'

'Let's all go,' suggested Hugo, and they took him at his word, all three of them heading for the front door, Beauchamp still holding aloft his tray with his drink, as yet un-tasted.

It was Lady Amanda who actually opened the door, peered out into the darkness, then shrieked one word, before clutching her hand to her heart. '*MUMMY*!'

Recovering at lightning speed, she added, 'But it *can't* be you, you're *dead*!'

A voice from out of the darkness, beyond the warm light spilling from the hall, spoke, as its owner took a step forward, to be recognised. 'Hugo, you've become fat. Manda, whatever have you done to the colour of your hair? It looks cheap and nasty! Ah, *Beecham*, a champagne cocktail. My favourite! How thoughtful of you.'

Beauchamp smiled as he held out the tray to her.

THE END

The Belchester Chronicles
by
Andrea Frazer

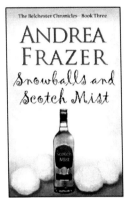
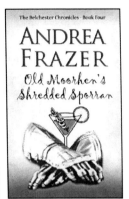

For more information about **Andrea Frazer**
and other **Accent Press** titles
please visit
www.accentpress.co.uk

Lightning Source UK Ltd.
Milton Keynes UK
UKOW04f1908191214

243443UK00001B/12/P